VIOLET AVENUE

Aaron Richard Golub

ALSO BY AARON RICHARD GOLUB

Feisengrad

The Big Cut

Ruckus

DEDICATION

To

my son Darrow, my inspiration

and

my parents, Charles and Esta Golub.

CONTENTS

CHAPTER 1

It was late August. It was like all waning summers, they pass so quickly you don't have time to towel off. The blueberries and strawberries taste bitter and I lose interest in just about everything, that includes myself. Then I crack like tree bark, from no other cause than my own inadequacies; call it in shorthand self-nothingness. When it happens, I leisurely walk down Violet Avenue, not exactly a shoppers' enclave and check into the Randolphe Hotel. It's an institution that has strict schedules, rules and a front desk. That's my special place and I really live there but no one knows that. This insanity takes on the punctuality of the swallows of Capistrano. The mind is noumenal in its functions, drives, breakdowns and I know from experience that there are no cures for mental illness. The manifestation is personality—the moods of the mind. How many times have I said, I'm in a good mood today? Don't start telling me about sanity or insanity; my least favorite word is juxtaposition. By the way, I never considered writing this in the third person.

So, I know nothing about myself and less about other people. I have great respect for anyone who has themselves "figured out" but who is that person and isn't it just another figure of speech? You figure. But the thing I need to know is why I go on this preordered craziness and now I have to figure it out.

At this point in August of that year, I had arrived at the solution—clean house, get rid of the women in my life and eliminate that thing called me. Focus on my law practice; after all, I am considered a top-notch New York City trial lawyer, which meant I spoke for others. The mass of confusion women provoked in my life had to end. I made up my mind that I was done.

What a cliché! As always, a woman escorted me—side by side—when I drew the drapes to my fall funk. My games, their intrigue, I was tired of it. But never forget that women are indispensable.

I was oblivious to every kind overture so why would I go down the wrong road? No, I wasn't looking for strange, because I was an alien to myself—peculiar as that man who is under the streetlight outside your apartment staring at you standing there alone with a whiskey tumbler in your hand. Are you afraid, should you invite him in?

When I conversed with them, I pretended to be involved but I didn't hear anything but static. Whatever I said—but the less I said—was intended to move us a step closer to the bedroom. Half the time I fell asleep. That's when the trouble began. Long-legged, beautiful women found me arrogantly fascinating. Intellectual women just didn't come my way.

Of course, I was accused of inadequacies. Case One said I was introverted, aloof. Case Two said I was cynical. Case Three said she hated men in their thirties but she doesn't have any idea how old I am.

Case Four happily introduced me to Case Five, who told me, "You look better in clothes. Never get undressed; damn, your body is ugly." Case Six said I was a bastard because I wasn't polite to cab drivers and waiters.

I was at peace with myself. There were no love-at-first-sight matches. No one danced the tarantella and gave me a spider bite, beside that Terry. But it was satisfying to know I was attractive to women. People called me an "ass man," which commanded respect in my college locker room. Women were dialing up my number, knocking at the door, writing letters, emailing, sending flowers. I was accosted by makeup, lingerie, long polished fingernails, sexy voices.

Then there was my fee based job. What's your fee...my fee is my vocabulary. All of it amounted to just a number, but I could've given up practicing law on five minutes' notice if something—a snippet of any job—better came along. Anything else I wanted to be I believed I could make happen.

I thought I'd be a good businessman but what business? I also wanted to be a professional athlete; I admired athletic prowess, especially poise under physical pressure, running around in a jock strap. Madison Square Garden was Temple Emanu-el to me (God be with us). My parents should've encouraged me to play sports but my mother was a happy college secretary, my father was a dedicated grocer, and they weren't sitting in the bleachers waiting for a slam dunk. I was a good athlete with a jump shot. Finally, there was only one narrow choice with two words: Practice law. Just about everyone who couldn't make their mind up about what to do with their life chose law—the profession of last resort. My hotel is a resort. Don't you forget it!

People made me medically sick, less my deductible. Satre (Jean Paul) said, "Hell is other people," for good reason. Most of the time I was either depressed or momentarily pleased with myself for winning a case, realizing what a great lawyer I was, especially when I argued with the bathroom mirror. Being good at a profession was momentarily rewarding. But I was much better than being good; I knew I was the best at something I hated doing but it put the rye bread on the breakfast table. My mother was very proud of that prick status but what she didn't know was that I suffered the contradiction of a Jew driving a Mercedes.

Boxers don't like to get punched and lawyers like everyone, hate adversity, but back then there was that kick from winning. Only those who overcome adversity succeed but no one ever told me that when I needed to know. I'd achieved success as a lawyer. Wherever I went I was recognized on my own account and talked about in my absence in painful laudatory terms for being "there goes that prick who can win."

The benefits to my clients were considerable. I was adept, eloquent, strong and I knew what the hell I was talking about. Sometimes I suffered the delusion I was a vigilante. The truth is weak adversaries made it so much easier. And I got clients what they wanted. Nothing else mattered to them. The state of New York gave me a license to make money. I paid for it with hard cash, seven years in undergraduate and law school listening to moronic lectures. I took their notes, I took their shit, then I took the piece of paper from the state that said I passed the test, then the certificate hung on my office wall and I charged by the hour. Every day since then I've shined my blade and stabbed files, phone calls, and lawyers.

Of course, it all worked in my favor and ultimately it drew her and me to the same place at the same time on a Sunday.

Was it just a week ago? I can't really recall when because of this hotel, its goddamn rules, its walls and its disinfectant smell. But I do get out once in a while because they don't have the staff to stop me.

But I digress. When you live in New York and you have the cash, taking a woman to upstate or Long Island for the weekend is standard practice. When you are in your thirties, what could be better than being in the country outside New York City with a tall beautiful blonde-haired woman for the weekend? You've arrived, you worked your ass off in Gotham, and it is well deserved. After a long freezing November walk on the beach, inside that craggy, weather-beaten rented beach cottage in the Hamptons, she's getting undressed in front of a crackling fire. It's all happening right after dinner and a bottle of French red. Your mind is flying and you're texting everyone you know in your head. It's just the two of you in the wild. Then just when you're staring at her thinking this is everything, reality sets in. Something in your brain tells you that you don't even like this woman and you know what—

she's thinking the same thing about you. You could get in your new sports car and drive straight back to the city and say good night. But you don't.

You have sex with her early in the morning because she lying on top of you breathing like a grizzly bear. She is fully participating, but your mind is someplace else—a Little League baseball game you played in twenty years ago when you struck out, bases loaded in the bottom of the ninth.

The day before, I had been in the country at my house. The phone rang when I was in my newly designed gambrel horse barn fifty yards from the wall phone in the kitchen, taking the saddle off my albino thoroughbred. It felt like a male-female relationship because I spent so much time riding her.

I didn't feel that way about the girl I'd once again brought up for the weekend. Muriel, call her my girlfriend. She was crazy about the bad way I was treating her. The first night we went out was the only time I was nice to her. I found out early, she was sensitive and loving but I wouldn't go down that road.

When I heard the phone ringing off the hook, I gave in, threw the girth and the saddle down on the barn floor and walked into the house. No need to hurry, anyone that called knew to let the house phone ring because I was always in the woods or in the barn where there was no cellular service.

It was Magritte Bollane, a married friend of mine who had a rented a country house about ten miles away. She and I planned during the week what we'd do on weekends; it was a ritual for us to get together for late afternoon lunches, dinner, horseback riding at dusk or boring each other and everyone else who was around to death with mundane conversation.

"Hello, Brane, we just arrived for the weekend. When did you get up?"

She was more outgoing, more certain of herself than any of the other married women I knew. There wasn't a time I recalled when she acted like a married woman. She led her own life and seemed, accidently on purpose, disconnected from Franco, her husband. But they had a noticeable bond, however strange the relationship seemed. She was a dark-eyed, raven-haired beauty, without that ridiculous fake air of alienation that beautiful women radiate. Her face had a beautiful pink and beige quality of a 16th-century old master painting that should have been on a canvas shipped from exhibition to exhibition. Instead, she was delivered from one dinner party to another by Franco, an odd man who had untrustworthy eyes, pointed features and a pernicious demeanor. It was a marriage that I secretly hoped would end in divorce—the sooner the better.

She went on. "There's a huge group of guests, many of them here for the first time." That raised my fresh-meat curiosity.

"Who?"

"Franco's over there. Let me see, I can pick them out one by one in the room: There's Radiance—you must know her. Radiance Tempest."

"No, I don't." I lied. I knew her vital facts and that she aroused men and women. Everyone in New York knows everything about everyone and fantasizes about what they don't know. I could see her face in white makeup pointing with her long fingers shellacked in pigeon blood red nail polish.

"They're chatting—Franco and Radiance—on the couch. Isn't it cold this weekend?" I was always cold around her, even on the phone.

"I should have brought my fur coat, it's freezing. Franco's clients are here in numbers and then there's a couple from London. Brita and Michael. I will be bored to tears unless you come over. Save me! Tonight, we'll have a great dinner; it will be fun only if you come."

I always felt an unmistaken chill when I was around Magritte but understood it as attraction.

"Sure, but I have Muriel with me this weekend; I haven't introduced her around."

I sounded like I wasn't planning to either, since any minute I was going to tell her to go back to New York City on the bus.

"Bring her, I love Muriel," Magritte urged, picking her way through my state of mind, and displaying compassion for the unintroduced Muriel. She'd heard the same tone in my voice so many times before. She was empathetic, I believed, tacitly acknowledging both of us were stuck in the dilemma of unwanted partners.

So, I agreed to come to dinner with Muriel. Any time Magritte invited me over, I went because she was damn seductive; I was attracted to her, but I couldn't gauge how deep it was—the range was just an affair to being in love with her. Curiously, I was afraid of her charm and scared to find out, so I strategically deflected some opportunities to be alone with Magritte. I made a joke out of every phrase that could lead to something more than idle socializing, turning away each time I sensed she was waiting for me to commit my eyes to hers, so I made certain she knew about my girlfriends.

It was easy to say yes to the invitation; I would do anything to break the monotony of sitting around my house with Muriel, gabbing aimlessly about the last case or lying about in bed with her, having her beautiful hands massage my unfeeling body. Her touch had long ago started to irritate rather than soothe me; even though I must have imagined it, when Muriel touched me, I felt pain.

But I excused it, suffered, because I hated being alone. During that summer I took her and my briefcase everywhere I went. That was unfair as hell because she fell in love with my cruel alienation. I watched this incredible beauty, this female perfection (except she had false teeth), become obsessed with me through the sole stimulation of my resistance. Her enslavement was

unbearable. At every turn all she wanted to do was please me into a furor—
to do what was my idea, my predilection, my crazy caprice.

On my birthday that year, she took me to dinner at a French restaurant
in Connecticut, where everyone was costumed in black tie, conversation was
no louder than a rustle of November leaves. Two hundred dollars just for an
entrée. After dinner she ripped my tux off in an empty banquet room. She
wasn't embarrassed, she wanted to please me to the max. She turned around
and leaned both elbows on a dining table.

"Take me, right now, from there, from behind me, grind it into me," she
moaned in complete rapture but in control. You don't easily locate women
who use the word grind seductively. A friend of mine was chairman of a
private company called The Grinding Concern but this undertaking was not
corporate. In that moment she knew how to get me out of my penguin suit
and into her.

But other than those rare occasions, the relationship droned. I felt like I
was carrying a thick book around that I'd never read. The pathetic part was
she knew it. At times I vacillated, felt sorry for her, but I could never forget
those women who treated me like shit, like Terry. My compassion for Muriel,
any woman, was limited knowing each woman I went out with destroyed
some other guy right before they met me.

Muriel was still in the barn removing the tack from my elegant white
mare, named Whitehall. I also had a black horse I called Blackhall that was
built like a draft horse. Nothing new in my black and white world. From the
kitchen window across the driveway, I watched her, suddenly confused,
reminding myself that I couldn't possibly be with anyone or anyone better.

Nothing mattered and nothing could be less important than beauty in
those moments. I knew my way around the void. Then I could see just her
hand, a lovely abstraction reaching for the towel hanging from the hook on
the wall, moving back to wipe the thick lather off the horses. We'd ridden a

long time that afternoon. Friends who rode with me complained later beer-drinking in the kitchen that we stayed out on the trails too long, but it was something I loved— listening to the compulsive sounds of hooves pounding against the ground like the rhythm of Dylan Thomas reading W. H. Auden's "As I walked out one evening," leaning over the side of my horse and jumping dangerously high stone walls. They were correct because I compensated for the lack of excitement in my life by rigorous riding; but I knew when to stop and when to convert my aggression back to something boring.

I continued to stare out the window. Efficiently as she could be, Muriel finished drying the horses, hooked both of them to a lead rope, and walked them around the circular part of the gravel drive until they cooled off. A few minutes later, she was finished. Who could ask for a better girlfriend? There she was the crack in the teacup. Now I feared we'd have contact, something I'd avoided all morning galloping in front of her on every trail. I struck a wooden match and planted a cigarette in my mouth, regarding Muriel resentfully as she led the horses to the paddock and walked toward the house. My mood was swinging and maybe I was in my room at the hotel. Here she comes. Now she was the peacetime foe and not to be rotten to her was my intention, but that was unnatural. After she entered the kitchen, she closed the door behind her gently as if something romantic floated in the air, maybe Cupid.

Then her arms opened wide, tentacles coming toward me, reaching for confirmation, for contact, for the sensation that everything is all right. That seemed so simple. I could force myself to do it but instead I moved out of the way and opened the refrigerator door.

"Do you want something to eat?"

"No, I want to kiss you, honey." She was tracking me like a bloodhound.

"No, not now. I am not in that mood." Although I wanted to add I hadn't been for months and I was always trying to squirm out of kissing her. But she wouldn't let me go that easily.

"Why don't you kiss me?" Her voice plaintive, sad, making lip contact even less appealing, call it irrelevant. Besides, the question "why" gave me the chance to explain all the sick things my mind was suffering from then and there, but I resisted. So, it wasn't just a subhuman avoiding one kiss with a human. I wasn't going to give her a thing physically. The face was there, immoveable, the Sphinx—her lips puckered, eyes closed tight, lids scrunched, panhandling me for a simple kiss. No, I just couldn't do it and how I hated being called "Honey." Sounded so goddamn cheap, worse than "Peaches."

She was swimming in space with her jaw guiding the way. She pulled back, frightened that all she was going to receive was something unexpected in the face—a wet sponge, discarded food, some practical joke. I shoved a piece of cheddar between her lips and laughed maliciously. Before I knew it, her right hand whipped around and slapped my smirking face. Instantly, I counter-slapped the air, missing her on purpose, but it sent her reeling against the GE dishwasher. At that moment, I calculated like a Greek grocer and concluded like an old prostitute that the relationship had another twenty-four hours to go, tops. Tears streaming down her face, hands in the air, she came at me feline-style. Her attraction for me put aside like a quart of sour milk. She was nothing but compiled anger, legs kicking and arms curving toward my head. She'd have to get credit for trying, but for the ten minutes or so the bellicosity lasted, I averted almost every one of her blows. We were not a match.

"You bastard, you son of a bitch...you are a shit," fired at me like a spliced laser. To her disadvantage she was Danish and those were the only English words that came to mind when she lost her temper. I had heard them before in the same order. A few of those punches landed; later I noticed black-and-blue marks flowering on each arm. In a strange way, I wanted to stand still—stop my life—and let her beat the hell out of me for all the times I'd been so brutish to her. I deserved it (I have a very good sense of fairness; I would've made a great judge) and she was badly in need of some satisfaction. Also, I might add just to confuse the situation, I was always too damn hard on myself. She didn't have to stay around all those weeks letting me step on her. So, I thought, "If I can act totally out of character this one time, maybe allowing her beat the crap out of me, that will serve a very good purpose—she won't get hurt when the relationship ends later this week."

The attack would have gone on longer than I can restrain myself except my cell phone rang. God knows it owed me a favor after all the rotten calls I'd received. I grabbed for it, the excuse to stop the fight. Magritte was phoning back.

"Hello, Brane, are you there?"

"Yes, yah, it's me." I pulled away from Muriel.

"I was just ringing back to tell you to make certain you bring Muriel, we have room. I don't know whether I made that clear. There's plenty of food but if you want you can bring some red wine."

Bobbing and weaving like a prizefighter who knows he's about to get nailed, I moved out of Muriel's range. The last thing I wanted was Magritte to hear what was going on, or to know anything personal about me so I muted the phone. I was living a ridiculous myth, a fantasy with Magritte. I was trying to give her the impression that I was the ideal example to measure her husband by, or any other man. Where do ideas like that come from? I liked Franco just a bit even though he had a phony Cheshire cat smile and greasy black hair. He didn't know what bullshit I was pretending to be, because I went through it like a paid actor.

I unmuted the phone, quickly inserted it into one of the small quiet areas between the screams and screeches of Muriel.

"I'll call you back in a few minutes," I clicked off and turned around to face combat once more. About eight feet away she stood still, round-shouldered, her head listing up and down like an ocean buoy, shaking. The soft side of me emerged—I walked to her, tried to kiss her moist, averted cheek.

"I am sorry," I whispered, "sorry." But she snapped her head away. The last vestige of her fallen pride, detritus scattered all over the kitchen floor. There wasn't any way to cloak the reality of how destroyed everything she'd hoped for had become. The emptiness of us walked through the center of the room like a bride in black. I thought about how many times I'd been here before—on the receiving side. Suddenly I began to feel terrible about her pain; I identified with it as if I were in the audience. Like an expert I knew the experience. I felt the urge to cry with her—side by side for our common tragedy.

A few minutes later, after we'd remained reverently silent and still, she tugged at the collar of her flannel shirt, using it to dry her eyes. One of the buttons popped, exposing her right breast. My eyes glanced sidelong into the open space and watched her nipples heave gently against the material. At the same time, the intensity of the battle between us began to lift. Confrontation is the most brilliant sexual stimulant. The fight's excitement was pulling me, temporarily, out of the hive of sexual lassitude. I reached inside her shirt and cupped her breast. The right one. For the first time that weekend I noticed her tan; she'd been in the Bahamas that week. All over again, as if we were meeting for the first time, I began to admire her beauty while my other hand's fingers were gently tripping along her back. Before I realized it I was holding her, kissing her neck, rubbing her shoulders, massaging her breasts and making the nipples into hard, stiffened, little sex switches.

The brawl was spinning into passion. We clutched each other. I acted the part of the army hero, she, the wife, meeting me on the wharf as I returned home from the war.

For the rest of the afternoon, we made love. In those days I could last for hours and forget about being a hypocrite.

About four-thirty, autumn's dusk materialized while I was trying to nap and she was fully awake, smoking menthol cigarettes, one after the other. Starting that month, I couldn't fall fully asleep because I was unable to concentrate, turn the dial to off. The answer to my problems was in dreams, forced fantasies. The brain introduced me to thousands of ugly characters starring in grotesque narratives. Yet what I wanted most was these peculiar experiences, this raucous sleep, knowing there wouldn't be a minute of peace. I became a masochistic addict, the body insisting on rest with dreams although I was never tired.

Around eight o'clock, I woke up. Muriel was sitting on the bed with her beautiful curved back against the wall, crushing out another butt with her profile between me and the moonlight. The light cascaded off the French windows, leaving her in contour. Everything pointed toward the end. I wanted that photograph, so I'd never favor the memory with anything but the truth—the brutal interlude, the Edward Hopper space between two people in their last moments together.

She nervously broke the silence. "I know you're awake. Are you still going to have dinner with your friends?"

For a moment I didn't reply, searching somehow for an expression which'd make it seem as if I wanted her to come. What I needed was a phrase that would be genuinely nice, though keeping the idea in clear sight that we were on our last hurrah. There wasn't anything I could think of to say that would describe our circumstances. Over and over again I wanted to tell her straight out that when we returned to the city I wasn't going to see her again.

"Yes, let's get dressed and get out of here. It'll be great to go out," I exclaimed, lying, emphasizing that I was more enthused about going out with her than going out.

"Brane, I don't feel like it. I don't. You go on without me." Her face turned away, self-distractedly. I extended my arm, pressed her hand and against my will said, "Come on. I want you to go with me. You'll like these people, you like Magritte, and we shouldn't be in two different places."

There was a long pause. Neither of us was tempted to say anything else. She was aware that I didn't want her to come but she couldn't say no.

"OK, I'll go, but I don't see any purpose," she relented.

We dressed. Saturday night was always an imposition, a night for socialization, a process of the week reserved for good times. When people ask, "Where did you get that suit?" My grandmother used to ask me the same question every time she saw me dressed up: "Where did you get that?" She was so poor she wanted to make certain that my clothes weren't stolen.

I pulled on an old pair of jeans, a vintage Ralph Lauren shirt, a brocade Chinese vest, an old hound's tooth coat that I bought at the flea market for fifteen bucks and a vintage pair of English riding boots. It's a good thing I didn't like jewelry. I finished dressing like a clown so I wouldn't recognize myself, which served that purpose considering my state of mind. Clothes meant nothing and everything to me. None of the pieces matched. So, what! Muriel thought I had a terrific wardrobe and she also loved my stale Art Deco surroundings. I lived in and around inlaid tables, deco prints of willowy Thirties women, ivory and bronze figurines, Tiffany lamps and Persian rugs. The goddamn collection looked like a thrift shop.

I put on a record of very depressing music, Eric Satie, "Gymnopédie," stood in front of the fireplace thinking about what I had left to do in life, smoked a cigarette down to the filter. Quitting is out of the question and I'll never vape that crap. Upstairs, Muriel was taking a bath, getting dressed and doing some other things to prepare herself for the battle of Saturday night. It was taking too long and it pissed me off.

I yelled to Muriel, "Waiting for women to pull themselves together is despicable. Thousands of my brilliant ideas are being sucked down the drain waiting for you to dress, make up, and do hair."

"Brane, relax, I'll be done in thirty minutes," she replied.

"Thirty goddamn minutes. All my poems, songs, beginnings of great novels, inventions, all being turned to the shit of waiting time," was all I could think about. I threw down a shot of scotch and dug out a bottle of red to take to the dinner.

CHAPTER II

That social stuff didn't develop out of nowhere. There is a backstory that should be told to put things in context. All my connections are a bridge to nowhere. My doctor said that and he also said I should stop kidding myself, but that would destroy all the fun and after all I know more about myself than anyone. Everyone sees only the outside, not the inside, and that's straight out of the Old Testament.

Growing up in Massachusetts I looked in my bathroom mirror every day and said to my outside self, "I'm normal."

I was able to stay healthy and did boyhood crap like fight with my parents, chase girls, play basketball, get expelled, had the first girlfriend experience, wore ripped Levi's and sweatshirts, smoked and drank beer. That's pretty normal.

Against all odds I made it through high school, college and even law school. Then came the time—when I turned twenty-one—when life-changing events took hold and I forgot all about normal.

By then I was in law school, deeply innocent, when I met Terry. This is where things got fucked up. After a short spell, I even believed she and I had a real love affair, starting right from the moment she jerked me off—saving me the labors of Portnoy—while I sat there dumbfounded on a black leather seat in her navy-blue VW convertible. But I realized over time spent strolling in the adult crosswalk the experience was wicked, not sexual. She was goddamn evil. It was her idea to go for that ride—she was in control—that sun-drenched fall foliage afternoon, although I met her when she dated my roommate. He was understandably crazy about her but I dismissed any sense of guilt because "I'm not interested in Charles," was the first thing she said to me.

There she was outside the law school, her engine idling just for me or anybody or any somebody that didn't come along. Serial sex killer. One instant you're nothing, the next you're on top of the world; how do these situations happen? Not usually with a devilish introductory hand job but that made me plunge right into her lagoon and her agenda.

Weeks later in winter, well after that ride, we were at a late Saturday afternoon law school cocktail party in Chapel Hill. There was that classic buzz between us. I was on one side of the room and she on the other, in the midst of a thicket of Southerners clocking shots of Early Times, Jack and coke, mixing. Every so often I'd look up at her dark eyes—they were meeting mine and all I could hear was "My Girl" by the Temptations. A match made in hell. We would always have that kind of communication, I thought, but in the end, that we-are-one feeling meant we played catch with my emotions. Nothing more.

In front of a river rock fireplace where *Y'all* had gathered there was a female law graduate talking about life. She'd been out in the cruel world and learned one thing.

"Life is selling," she barked like a German shepherd, ignoring the hearth's dangerously high flames, making her point to a crush of wide-eyed students. They would find out standing in their cuffed khaki pants that she was right. Practicing law is selling argument, more often than not, baseless persuasion. At that second when the word "selling'" jackknifed out of her matriculated mouth, Terry and I again focused on each other as if we knew a higher truth that wasn't so mundane because we had naïvely planned our hopes and dreams without factoring in the evil world of selling. When we were alone, we laughed like hyenas at how damn different we were, the Yankee and the

Southern belle, Fitzgerald's "The Ice Palace," but we almost matched because I sold myself to her and she sold herself to me, but there I was selling out.

It was a lie that we understood more than anyone there, but seconds later Terry lowered herself, disappointing me, talking to some pimply preppy, good old boy from her hometown who "knew her daddy well." Women do that just when you think you've got the unattainable one. There she goes to the bar, enraptured by some schmuck.

I turned my attention to a guy in my torts class who lured me into a golf rap. That was another contradiction. I went from being a sharp Northerner who wore pegged pants and dark vests to a nerd who played eighteen holes of golf on the school course after federal tax class, wore alpaca sweaters, banana yellow cuffed pants and carried a new golf bag. Don't ask me how I was converted from a Bean Town hipster to a Southern duffer.

What I should have done at that party was stride across the room, take her by the hand into the bathroom, pull her wool slacks to her ankles and go down on her. But I behaved. Terry did, too, even though that was what she wanted, what she craved every afternoon right after class. The goddamn trouble with our relationship was her unwillingness to let go of the South. My focus was going down on her and I could care less about the North. When things were right, her mission was putting the best part of me in her mouth—connecting my pipe to her drain. The cherry on the cake was she was crazy. There is nothing as great as sex with a psychopath—it is the highest of the high. There is no next level.

After all, there wasn't anything so unique about my obsession. Every guy wanted her. But no one fucked her because she had that dated stop sign, no intercourse until I am married. No trespassing. There wasn't anything overtly sexy about her but she was seductive and better yet, sultry. The soft round face, her thin lips, the sharp cheekbones teased the hell out of me. Her hair was prematurely gray, she wore bright colored cotton skirts, canary yellow flats, and white lace shirts. That combination was sensual, sexy, provocative. All of it made her unpredictable. I never knew when she'd give me the green light.

She'd squeakily ask, "Do you think I have a beautiful forehead? You know, like Italian Renaissance paintings of courtesans?" Courtesans, what? I automatically answered "Yes." It took time before I saw those paintings but she knew them well.

Culture aside, finally I understood Terry sucked just for the sake of sucking. What a fraud; I thought we were in a mutual receiver-giver relationship. The act wasn't performed to increase my satisfaction; she just loved it for the one-sided pleasure it gave her. I could've been a department store mannequin that she attended as No. 6 who ordered me, No. 9. It happened like clockwork every day after school, sucking from paycheck to paycheck at 4 p.m. She never told me that our appointments wouldn't include fucking. I had to find out on my own after months of thinking, some day or night, I'll make love to her.

I was on the short end of orgasm. She'd slip out of my grasp and lickety-split she'd be down there sucking as a consolation prize. Each time her legs locked up like a bank vault. Her vagina was the storeroom of family guilt: her father's conviction for embezzlement, her mother's alcoholism, her brother the queen and her sister's nymphomania. Resistance to what the outside world wanted from her would rectify all those transgressions.

Not getting laid can be dangerous and the rejection was painful. The desperation, the desolation she caused pushed me to the limit, to the roof of the empty law school on a Sunday morning. Off the elevator, through the stacks and out onto the slate roof. The night before she had a date with someone, a guy in the second-year class, the one behind me. I drove by his apartment. Two silhouettes on the shade at 2 a.m. Her car parked in front. Damn it! I could almost hear her in there sucking furiously as if one were being devoured by a pterodactyl! All night I sat like a statue in my car, waiting, self-pitying tears running down my twenty-one-year-old cheeks.

Early that morning I stood on the edge of the roof and looked down at the concrete steps imagining the feeling of my body smashing into pieces. Then, at last, that esoteric mechanism in the brain, which waits until the last second, chimed in, "Stop, don't do it. She's not worth it, she's full of shit." I agreed.

So, I climbed down the steps, got back into the car and at least, I'd proven that suicide was out. Big deal. She wanted me to go crazy. She relished my torment. Me walking around mad as a hatter and everyone saying, "She did it, she flipped him."

"Actually, she's just an old-fashioned cocksucker," Charles said when it was over. But I never learn any lessons. Whatever I know I never apply to my circumstances.

I read *The Blue Angel* as a tutorial on lust. I was young then but I understood the craving Terry put me through.

I knew this was something else, not early romance, and I knew one sunny day I'd be gazing out a window wondering where it went. Funny, I even looked forward to that day and that window.

Anyway, there was more than one lesson in Terry but everything I learned transformed my small supply of optimism into cynicism. Now I spend my time caring for the diseases of my mind, trying not to contract new ones.

It ended during the last minutes of a fiery red sunset closing a beautiful day. I was drunk, angrier than usual, standing on the blacktop roadway leading to the back of the law school. Terry was inches from face while I braced myself against the hood of my convertible Dad was paying for, staring at a woman that would soon be gone forever.

Law school was over and I would never see the hills of North Carolina again. My hunger for her would go unfulfilled. Minutes before, back at my pink house in the woods, my classmates (the ones who weren't anti-Semitic) and I had celebrated the last final exam and I packed for the trip north.

I futilely tried to say the right thing to her.

"You're a whore, unfaithful—"

Right then she cut me off and drawled, "I know this. . .this thang we had is over."

What an understatement! That *thang* we had was a year of nonstop sex and that's an accomplishment in anyone's book.

She went on, flooring her accelerator, loving every word,

"I knew you had one more examination, so I had to see you for the last time before you left here."

I reminded her of my favorite verb and noun, "You fucking whore!"

"I don't mind being called a whore, I like the sound and it excites me," she unabashedly answered with one hand on her hip like a 42nd Street hooker. Whatever I wanted to call her it was perfectly fine.

"Brane, you knew from the beginning we were unsuited for each other." What?

She'd segued into her lifestyle routine that she would bring up from time to time.

Unsuited, what a fucking word. I was being dumped on terminology, catchall phrases.

As you will see I am still alone and so is she now, no longer married. Like I said we lost it, the sex, the laughter and the eye contact. The relationship became rough, turbulent, bruising. She went insane, went to the psychiatrist, went to a hospital, and married some good old boy from her hometown (population 25,000), faded into the impenetrable Southern weave. Now

I heard rumor she lives alone in a white shingled country cottage with a cat. All the conflicts between us were not healed over time. I wanted to get even with her but that's immature. Now I know we didn't understand one another except in the main arena—sex.

Since the last incident at the law school, I've called her every so often. She claims that she doesn't know me, my calls are "hostile," which was consistent with her past claims that my erections were a sign of hostility. I don't think she'd understand me now or my poems. Everyone at the hotel compares them to William Shakespeare. They must be crazy. Here's a good one.

Overhead Cobra

Overhead cobra
smiles.
The side of its head
holds a congenital mouth of
minstrel teeth, attached by nothing.
Six reflection of mean, Second World
War
Japanese approach in shadow
Phantasmagoric, is it ww2?
Or are they hallucinations that
could simply be found in knotty pine?
Diamond-shaped opening of the snake's
mouth; the Japs come more clearly into
focus; cherry red lips, square teeth

growing up and forward like rhubarb,

green slices of odd food caught in

the nostrils and between the teeth,

And,

then my concentration was run down

by a fiery sports car coming up to the

side of me from over the up and down

bridge, wide as a sales slip. The

car and the driver are ablaze but he

stops at the service station. The attendant

holds out a fuel hose; hammers, sickles,

swastikas and scimitars—

gold plated—pour out, all over the pavement.

CLANG

A giant black god longs for service,

looks both ways angrily; no one is coming.

And then the eagle stands up, halfway . . .

the possessor of the dream's answer.

Restful God, galloping God, cloven-hoofed God,

God's legs are broken now; now just an aging goat;

legs running backward like lake pipes.

God appears from under the eagle, checked by a

chicken wire enclosure.

And there you go watching half of my

face is a rat and the other half is me

thinking I was way ahead

The Hotel Randolphe is one place someone like me can go and not just for a
visit. Everyone lives in one hotel or another. Does the hotel exist? I don't
know but I seem to regularly check in. Is it the place I reside when I engage

in the discourse of another universe? Nearly every day when I get here I sit on my bed, wipe my forehead dry, running my right thumb across it like a windshield wiper. I sweat, no matter what the temperature. It must be old age, anxiety, all of it.

Maybe I'll meet someone in the hotel who will slip me a Lexapro, take me sailing around the world or we'll just go for a walk around the park. The pharmacy next door, I'll go there and meet a pretty girl from the neighborhood who's getting her prescription filled.

Why do I want to come back here? Because I'm connected to this hotel; after all these years I return as if I were on a swivel. It wasn't that long ago I moved in for the first time. I can still feel that grimy, unpolished brass-plated doorknob turning in my hand. The front door unexpectedly flew open and a bunch of kids ran by me like a flock of seagulls; well maybe they weren't kids. If I hadn't jumped out of the way, I would've tumbled back down the steps. After I had pulled the door open again and stepped inside I walked down a short hallway to Reception. On the right side of the room was a small desk, a rack of colorful postcards, and a beveled-edge sign that read: "Registration."

A clerk with aqua eyes, uncombed blond hair, and a toothbrush mustache sat there holding a pen as if he were expecting me. Everything told me this wasn't a difficult place to get a room. I signed the register. Without being asked to identify myself or produce my passport I paid the rate in advance just when he began to speak as if I were a complete stranger.

"This is The Hotel Randolphe, you will be in room thirty-one . . . a small, pleasant surrounding with a balcony overlooking the park. It's on the top floor." Beethoven's Ninth could be heard in the distant background, and I thought he used the word assigned.

"Top floor." That meant steps; there is no elevator in the hotel. His voice was jittery, nervous. There is always a tenseness between me and hotel personnel. This was no exception.

"Can I see the room first?" I asked, although I had already paid and knew the room well. It is a thing I always do, even at the best hotels. If I don't like it, then I check out.

"Certainly," he said, bowed slightly out of a sense of misplaced respect and rose from his desk.

We went on a tour of the entire hotel. The corridors had the faint smell of alcohol and diethyl ether. Every room was painted white and so were the hallways. So damn unnecessary. He must have taken into account my polluted state of mind. All the rooms were fully visited, even the ones with guests sleeping or arguing with their roommates or in bed watching television.

"Thirty-one will be fine," I said, not indicating I knew the premises after he showed it to me, even though the shower and the sink were strangely adjacent to a portable closet.

"I can get used to anything by now." He was expressionless because he'd heard that before.

"I think I'll enjoy my stay here at The Hotel Randolphe," I said to him as we returned to the desk, not revealing that my mind needed a long rest.

"You can call me Hans," he replied and I thought he said hands and for that I was grateful; I was in good hands. In fact, Hans looked like he could be a doctor, maybe even a psychiatrist.

After the tour he slipped around the desk like a gust of wind and reached up for the peg board, picking off a set of keys—one to a private mail box, the other to room thirty-one. My hand went into my pants' pocket, nervously searching for the first night's rent.

"You have already paid, it's been taken care of for some time," he said, reminding me that my stay was indefinite. I thanked him. Then I started for the steps.

"Remember … this is The Hotel Randolphe— never say The Randolphe Hotel." He advised me as if it were a standard finishing touch after a massage.

That was a warning I realized later, keep it all here in the hotel. Suddenly I became very obedient, went up to Room Thirty-one, unpacked, and neatly hung everything I owned in the closet. I felt a certain self-respect from getting along with Hans. Or maybe I wanted to feel like a well-mannered child who sleeps over at a friend's house.

As I unpacked, I realized I'd brought too many things. I thought I'd gotten rid of so much, but clothes are full of sentiment so they must be kept and when I leave Violet Avenue I have to carry them back.

The idea of living in a hotel was mine, wasn't it? It'd get me away from everything I own, to finally rent. My suitcase contained three pairs of pants, ten white shirts, two pairs of shoes, one pair of sneakers, and two pairs of cowboy boots that I never wear. I don't have a horse. Another bag was filled with reference books and dog-eared novels I intended to finish but were now fated to travel without another page being turned.

A day went by. No sooner had I begun to become used to thirty-one, or was it 31, that I was greeted with the first piece of bad news. Nothing is ever perfect. The woman in Thirty-two was sick. She couldn't stop her bronchial cough, and her crying was practically constant. I realized hotels were like automobiles: You can pick a lemon. And I came here for a rest, to be naked of the imperfect world I left behind.

This hotel was supposed to provide me with the absence of atmosphere, with a vacuumed vacation. Instead, hour after hour, the cough and the crying, her confluence of her maladies went on and she never shuts off the television because she is deaf. I found that out later. She knew at eighty-three she was dying and that this time it is not as her physician said "merely a virus." The walls were paper-thin. I could hear her clearly and I was able to imitate her as if her sounds were my own. Survival was important in my state of mind and I listened carefully. As for her, I wished her a peaceful death and an end to her suffering.

In the afternoon of that first day, around three, there was a rapping at the door. Hans. I was invited for tea in the hotel kitchen. What a privilege!

"Did that mean it'll be added to the monthly bill?" I asked. Thirty English breakfasts or other fragrant teas this month at one dollar per invitation. For a moment I thought about what to wear to tea. My white suit had been just pressed and hung in the closet. Everyone was wearing white.

"It should at least be worn once this season," I thought.

"Tea in a white suit in the early afternoon light, so goddamn English safari. Ridiculous!" I said to myself and went straight to the kitchen as I was in my robe.

Hans had taken a liking to me. After the second paper cup of a perfumed tea, he related a portion of the hotel's history. The professor who resided in the basement of the hotel's annex originally had said he would need the room for only fourteen days. "Well, it is just to check some scholarly papers for the university."

That was some six months ago. Of course, Hans was too polite and too disinterested to ask him what university he meant, because there wasn't one anywhere near the hotel.

Whatever! The most important thing to Hans was that the professor was not a dullard, which was good for the hotel. There has to be a good mix of residents. Once a day he went out, returned, and mentioned to Hans that the zoo across from the park (the hotel was on the cusp of a park) was full of animals who slept too much.

The professor was once a globetrotter, making judgments at international venues about the Armageddon, about which he said, with professorial certitude, "Like all things it will happen." He was not well.

Certainly, the professor knew the importance of saying "The Hotel Randolphe."

Later, as Hans left the room, I saw the stationer deliver to the front desk a box of writing. It had the professor's letterhead, in care of the hotel. In fact, he had resided here more than six months, longer than it takes to use one box of hotel stationery.

The woman's cough in thirty-two grew worse. I was afraid she'd vomit her trachea onto my doormat. Picture that tube on the carpet. Once through my door, I heard her say to Hans, "Yes, today I am going to the doctor, then I will feel much better." Hans was silent but I could imagine him smiling at her with his German lips and badly capped teeth. It was the first time I understood that if Hans lost his sense of humor, we'd all be in trouble.

When we were leaving the kitchen, Hans told me about a woman in twenty-two. She was not sick like my neighbor in thirty-two. I'd passed her on the way to my room. Her body was without description, I observed, concluding that these parts of the anatomy were brand new. Seventy-five was her approximate age and she wore only lingerie that came in boxed sets from a store in Paris where young girls shop.

Every day, Hans said, this woman from twenty-two was in the corridor with her porky legs walking her around on the well-worn plum carpeting.

The rest of her on top was clad in those French undergarments. Since then I have seen her both ways—clothed and nude. Her urine-colored hair crept up her skull like a caterpillar colony. Her skin was translucent, appearing as if scrubbed excessively with a coarse washcloth. Her feet were crammed into clear plastic, open-toe high-heeled shoes displaying her unclipped, gray toenails.

Who am I to make such judgments? I have to live with these tenants.

Only certain times of the month did she leave The Hotel Randolphe—once every third Thursday to confer with her attorney about estate matters; and Tuesdays to be coiffured by a young hairdresser, one hundred yards from the hotel. For these appointments she traveled back and forth only by radio taxi, she said, but I saw the ambulance. When these worldly events outside the hotel were over, her existence was simply reduced to residence in her room.

The drip from the showerhead ran constantly. She didn't mind. For years, as she explained to Hans: "I am always getting ready, whether or not I am clean. I will shower later, under the drip." Is that high sarcasm, because the shower doesn't work?

Each day at nine-thirty, Hans or one of the boys doubling as a chamber man brought breakfast to her room (a service provided exclusively for her): two hard-boiled eggs, one slice of burnt toast, a pot of American instant coffee, and two bars of bittersweet chocolate. Everything is eaten except the chocolate, which she crumbled into bits the size of guano, then spread it uniformly across the hotel's sterling silver breakfast tray engraved with her initials. Meanwhile, the mink coat she had custom-made in Rome (around the time of Mussolini, she claimed) hangs on the neck of the showerhead. The coat is still in good shape from the moisture, Hans claimed and said: "She knows how to care for mink."

On many nights she invites me for dinner and I play along because she's quite odd, probably crazy. Just to please her I eat the Belgian chocolate even though it is in fractured little pieces and I'm served quail eggs that I stuff in my pocket, pretending that they were delicious. We talk about literature. She loves Fyodor Dostoyevsky, Philip Roth and Thomas Mann.

At six o'clock on weekdays she orders two Coca-Colas and one beer. On weekends at six o'clock she orders two Coca-Colas and three beers. Twenty-five drinks a week and not a drop left in any of the bottles. Once per month this woman goes on an eating rampage, consuming five pounds of pickled herring, ten bleached-out sponge cakes, one dozen Danishes, one box of cream-filled candies and, lastly, she drinks twenty-four pints of dark beer. All of that gluttony takes place on a Saturday evening in twenty-two when I am invited to just keep her company.

"I do not pour one drop of beer down the drain nor flush a piece of food down the toilet," she told me. Her back and stomach flutter like aspic. After she eats I see her running around the landing in her creamy white satin and silk underclothes. Her thighs have the diameter of a manhole.

When she had signed the register of The Hotel Randolphe, she had told Hans, "I will be staying just fourteen days." I don't think it was up to her.

Years have passed. Her bills are paid promptly through the office of her attorney. She is always angry in the morning with the hotel's cat. She scolds it, regularly, for not eating its dried meal. Her kitchenette stinks from a cat's litterbox, going all the way back to the oldest cat that had moved out or died years ago, she told Hans.

"Do you think we humans should waste good money on cat food for such a one as you who does not even like to eat somesing?" She asks me and the cat every week in German.

The hotel does not have a cat.

Anyway, I still think The Hotel Randolphe is a fine place for people like us, even though Hans also informed me, after I finished drinking my second pot of tea, "Most of the guests die here." It was then that I noticed he had such a nice, undertaker's smile. Secretly, I call him "Digger." What do I care about that name after I'm dead?

The hotel is OK, I've said many times, but I am growing to hate the place; it's depressing. There is no red, flock-embossed wallpaper, like a whorehouse. That's my taste. They always let the tenants decorate the rooms if they're going to be staying more than a month but they can choose only one color: white. Hans told me that, too. My bathtub was embedded with the dross of every guest's sloughed epidermis dating to 1850, when the hotel was founded. The white curtains match the white walls. The bed was supported by shaky legs. There were two windows with dirty sills. Maybe the grime could be removed with a power sander. White violations.

All of this was not my fault, nor Hans', for that matter. The policy was simply not to clean the rooms for guests. You take over where your predecessor left off and you do the cleaning.

I moved in a few months ago, recommended by a friend of mine who had occupied this very room. Not a girlfriend, but I did sleep with her once, though not here. I know everything there is to know about her. I even knew when Thirty-one would be available. She had an incurable disease.

"So wait for me to die," she said. "And you can have my room."

In my way, I had a love affair with her. During her sickness I hadn't seen her, until she moved into the hotel. Late at night, she called and asked me to come over because she couldn't stand being alone. Very few people can. So, I went there and found out she was dying right then. I felt like I was talking to Jean Harlow or to some other great screen beauty and that terrible night I pretended to love her. That's the safest time to love anyone—when you know they're about to die. We matched. During her life I would never have considered it. I was not going to fall in love with her or anyone else. Furthermore, I'm not the type of person who uses the word "love" often, and when I say it, I clearly define it for my listener.

CHAPTER III

We got into the car; by then, Muriel was in the mood for stepping out. Spreading across her face was an "I'm in love with you" smile and her left hand was rubbing my right thigh. Isn't life grand? I shifted into fourth gear, va-voomed the accelerator and ignored her. She moved closer, unzipped my fly, trying to unbutton those tawdry vintage jeans. I was driving up the long, winding, tulip-tree-lined, gravel driveway to Magritte's house and I wasn't resisting. Around the side was a small parking area in front of a four-car garage. I inched into a space between the other cars and I looked down at Muriel sucking me off before dinner as if we were kids at a drive-in movie. I lit another cigarette and thought about how I was going to talk about this someday. Through the kitchen and dining room windows I could see a guest of Magritte's preparing food, looking in our direction, and another person bringing in firewood from the yard. That's when I came in Muriel's mouth. But she didn't stop. The blow job segue of the night was over with and she had the nerve to try to make me come twice. That wasn't happening.

"Muriel, c'mon let's go in. I think they are preparing to serve dinner."

"Umm, umm," she moaned, swallowed and said,

"I don't like going there. I think they—Magritte and Franco—are so damn weird."

"Weird? You're crazy. Magritte and Franco are fun. Magritte loves you, don't worry about it, you've known them for a while," I replied.

I put the cigarette out and clicked off the radio. Damnit, Muriel started all over again and there was no way I wanted that to happen. Bet she was doing it on purpose, to drain every bit of desire out of me, sensing that there had to be another woman at the dinner party to whom I might be attracted.

"C'mon baby, let's go. I really don't want you to do that again and I don't like being rude, they must know we're out here," I grabbed her shoulders and pulled her away.

Of course, I didn't give a shit about rudeness; I am a coarse bastard and I also don't give a damn about stopping a girl from getting what she wants. I don't abide by that stupid double standard that men have to fight for every sexual inch they get from a woman, but men are not supposed to resist a woman's aggressiveness. Women have the nerve to be hurt when they're rejected!

She didn't react. Her hand twisted the rearview mirror, she applied a shade of pink lipstick and brushed her hair as if nothing happened.

We walked around for a few seconds. The navy gray wood-framed house with its gables and dormer windows shaded by striped awnings was built in the Sixties. It was a beauty.

The backyard was landscaped to death, a flat, grassy plateau off the veranda enclosed by privet shrubs; behind, the land sloped down to a small cabana and swimming pool. There was a barn and paddock with horses ambling along the fencing. Magritte and Franco rented the place to entertain on weekends. They really had no interest in taking advantage of the country except for occasional long walks and throwing parties. Everything was for the moment, a place to go in Westchester on weekends.

Magritte answered the door. As we moved inside, she gave Muriel a kiss on the cheek and I handed her the bottle of red wine.

"So glad you could come," Magritte said to Muriel, as she hung our coats in the foyer closet.

I avoided the living room. By the time I turned around, Muriel was already being chatted up by a gold-buttoned, blazer-jacketed Wall Street type. Meanwhile, I didn't want to meet anyone just yet. I hate being introduced so I stumbled into the kitchen, bumping into a beautiful woman slicing red peppers. At first, I couldn't see her face except in profile. Her hair was short, straight to the point, very German.

She turned, sliced a tomato and bent her head in my direction, wiped her thin hands dry and smoothed the sides of her terry-cloth apron.

"Hello, I'm Biata. You must be Magritte's friend Brane," her hand came toward me. "Sorry, I like shaking hands."

"You are?" I asked, pretending to be a nice guy, also extending my hand.

"I'm Biata. I'm certain I just said that. We are here for the weekend with my two sons. Many times, Magritte has invited me for the weekend. It is so relaxing in the country."

The problem is I don't listen when I'm introduced. A serious tone was in her voice.

For a moment Biata and I stared at one another. An attraction? Hardly, but we felt something in common about the jagged spectrum of life. My eyes narrowed, at first out of nervousness, then they felt like railroad tracks becoming a single line in the distance, zeroing in on her age, her looks, her life difficulties. Although her skin had a youthful quality, she was over thirty. Her body was fit.

She sounded automatic, cold, talkative.

"Probably we would have met before, weeks ago, when I was here last, but I was told you were away and I have been in Europe often since both of my sons are in school in Switzerland."

Then she looked at me as if something was bothering her, abiding by the rule that one confides in complete strangers.

"There's a few other matters I take care of over there . . . which I am certain are of no interest to you."

I waited for her to say what was on her mind; who she went over there to screw (or whatever she did abroad) was of interest to me and made more than the slightest difference. Maybe she was trying to be intriguing. But it sounded like a matrimonial problem and I could smell divorce. Maybe it was just more of the complex, ponderous German manner that I was misinterpreting. The subject was changed to my profession, which underscored a legal issue.

"You're a lawyer. There were some legal things that had to be cleared up when we rented the apartment in the city and Magritte suggested I call you. But she said that you really didn't handle real estate matters, so I called a friend of my father's, who took care of it. He didn't charge us. The whole thing didn't take long."

Just what I expected, the story wasn't very sexy. I lost interest because there was no money and the law is a sexless subject.

"You're a New York City lawyer?"

I'd been asked those questions ten thousand times in my years of practicing law. How the hell can people not know I'm a lawyer in New York City, damn, just look at me! I reek office building and copying machine. After a deep breath the words flowed out like social vomit.

"Yes, that's it, yes, I practice law in New York City."

"Go on."

"But . . . being a lawyer is dull," I threw boredom into the mix.

Well, dull wasn't the right response, but then again, I was sure whatever I said wouldn't make any greater difference to her existence than the cucumber in her hand. Anyway, I was defending myself and the league of hip lawyers, who are full of shit; you know, the ones the magazines listed as the new breed or the top ten lawyers in the world. Yes, the legal profession was on my nerves; I'd grown to feel like I was canned argument.

Then for no reason I shifted into gear, looked her in the eye and put it on her, "I am a trial lawyer. Let me tell you a story."

"If you insist," she sighed politely. Usually people say I must have some good stories; she was clearly bored.

The blood rushed to my head because I knew I was about to sound off.

"At nine-thirty in the morning on my way to court yesterday, there I was going down FDR Drive in the back of a taxi with my client. We had discussed the case, he was a certified public accountant. I'd prepared for three days and three lugubrious nights in the Bar Association law library on West Forty-fourth, reading and interpreting cases and statutes. My client was my key witness—after all, it was his case. So, we pulled in front of the courthouse and all this time I am explaining the lawsuit, prepping him, the facts, his testimony. Both of us are carrying briefcases and dressed in suits ready for battle."

"Brane, excuse me, but is this really necessary?" she asked, stunned at my odd rant. So what, I went roaring on.

"Yes, it absolutely is, let me finish. I want you to know what being a New York City lawyer is all about." My voice was loud and obnoxious.

"Enter the halls of justice, where controversies are stamped 'adjudicated,' decided by biased men and women in faux Roman courthouses that have facades that say 'Knowledge Is Power' and inside there is a sign that says, "Men's Room Second Floor." Signs everywhere."

"Huh?" Biata tried to interrupt, as confused as a turnip landing in the wrong salad.

"Let me tell you, there is no one else to trust. My client and I waited for the elevator; he pulled my arm and whispered,

"When I testify, I'll lie, cheat . . . do anything . . . any fucking thing to win this case."

The client said a minute later, "I don't give a shit about breaking the law, I don't give a sweet fuck about God, the oath is a truckload of bullshit to me."

When the word "God" came out of his mouth, his head lurched back, his eyes nervously scanned the ceiling. He acknowledged that even the "truckload of bullshit" was owned by God's trucking company.

Then without looking back for her reaction, I started to walk out of the room but abruptly stopped, said to myself, "You're crazy. What the fuck was that about? They'll put you away." Chalk that up to my fall insanity.

"Oh, I forgot something. I left it in the car."

That was a lie to get me out of there. I turned around and started for the front door.

"Why don't you go through this door; isn't your car parked there? It's closer."

Biata pointed to the nearby kitchen door to the garages. I recalled she'd seen us through the kitchen window when we parked. Now it felt certain she knew Muriel went down on me. Was that why she chatted me up?

I smiled because I knew what to do (she saw everything). Then she returned to the counter, scooped up some vegetables and finished making the salad as if nothing had happened.

When I returned to the kitchen she was gone. The dining room was noisy. The table was being set by another woman and Biata; they were speaking in German but I wanted to finish our conversation—explain my fucked-up self. However, I was ignored.

I thought of Muriel by elimination. Yes, poor Muriel. I knew I was being rude, adding to the stack of disrespect, throwing Muriel to a crowd of people, most of whom I hadn't met. I turned and walked down the hallway, through a small sitting room and stood on the steps leading down to the living room. Two women were playing backgammon. Closer to me, there were empty sofas opposite one another. A wood-burning fire was roaring, and the room was brightly lit—a perfect setting for confrontation. I played with the idea of pursuing Biata during dinner for no good reason.

Muriel was seated alone. A couple sat opposite her reading the *Sunday Times*. In the armchairs, two Europeans were discussing in French the problem of the Swiss franc and the common market, their hands moving, their heads tilting and floating as if they were drowning in the English Channel. The room looked like Madame Tussauds Eurotrash wax museum.

The other guests were upstairs getting dressed. As a rule, Franco came down for dinner last, pasty-faced, his black hair slicked extra tight to his skull that introduced his small but very noticeable widow's peak, that he claimed he inherited from his Italian grandfather, Count So and So. His eyes were darkened by mascara; he wore a black tailored tuxedo jacket with tails, his thumbs placed behind its red silk peaked lapels. This was his stage entrance. I let the whole pretention pass, although I was full of wisecracks; I stored it alongside the other inexplicable inhuman Franco behavior I'd witnessed, never really wanting to ponder the totality of Franco's twisted self-image of the strange host who despised entertaining but enjoyed scaring people.

Franco twisted his mustache slightly, looked over the dinner guests as if they were on the menu, tightened his lips, brushed one palm over the other. Under the soft lights overhead he moved to the head of the table as the room quieted.

"Good evening, welcome to our country home. I am so pleased to meet new people who can add new dimensions to our thinking. Let's eat and be thankful. The fish will be getting cold, don't wait for me to start," he added curiously as he had kept everyone waiting for an hour.

The forks move through the air like bows across violins toward the Dover sole, accompanied by bottles of Château Lynch-Bages, 1996, not the funky red I brought.

Magritte often thought she had too much responsibility heaped on her for Franco's social sports. She expended incredible energy cooking Italian meals, making herself sexy and cleaning up after the barbarians chowed. Going back before Franco, she was an actress doing theater in the West End of London and beginning to get her "first breaks." There was a career in television along with a movie or two each year in which she could play anybody from a nineteen-year-old to a member of the English upper class.

Instead, Magritte opted for Franco's Teflon life. Every so often she'd take out her photo album and show me the pictures from her acting career.

I was a spectator; now momentarily during dinner I considered Magritte as a springboard for getting me out of this mess with Muriel. My brain was a flickering monitor searching for a nonexistent channel. Dinner was over. I observed the activity in the room, which revolved around the same two women playing backgammon. I told myself that neither one of them was my type but one of them was the infamous Radiance Tempest.

Someone had pointed her out in a restaurant about a year ago. I formed an impression of her. She was always with an entourage, an interesting straggler with no apparent purpose. Somehow everyone in that crowd looked as if they, like scales on a crocodile's back, were part of something bigger and each one was a component part. Was she a great beauty or flat-out hideous looking? What made her interesting was her fucked-up background and a permanent scowl stretched across her weather-beaten, pallid face. The nose curved back, talon like. Maybe she wasn't evil; she'd just had a rich girl's hard life and taken a lot of prescribed drugs to get through it.

What happened took place too long ago for most people to remember, except some society alcoholics who frequented places like The Union Club or The Racquet Club. Her father was a rich playboy, European, but the money was made in America by his stepfather. Rumor had it they lived in a strange estate that looked haunted, and someone said that when one spent the night there, "They were living very fast."

He raced cars, climbed the face of Mt. Highest Peak and went to the bottom of the sea in a diving bell to some record depth and on and on until the death wish, the challenge, was amply fulfilled when he sped off the track behind the wheel of a burgundy Maserati. The car roared up an embankment, careened off a concrete wall, flew through the air just in time for a telephone cable to decapitate him in front of 100,000 racing fans in the south of France. The Maserati plowed into the stands taking the lives of several spectators, including children; thirteen fans all told.

He knew he was defective before he belted himself in at the last pit stop. The right rear tire was rubbing against the wheel well. It was about to explode. But he was in the lead and that was important.

When she was ten years old her mother told her what happened while she was adjusting the plastic hands of her Madame Alexander doll at the funeral, realizing she would never hold her father's hand again. There would be many nights when she'd wake the guy she was sleeping with to tell him that tear-jerking tale.

"Throngs of racing fans lined the streets of Antibes, the procession was long, deeply populated. They were burying a national hero, my father. I can still feel those tears, trickling down onto my dress."

Magritte came up behind my chair, surprising me.

"Brane, have you met everyone?" she asked, the guests I hadn't met politely turning to me except for Radiance. She concentrated on rattling the backgammon dice box—that percussive sound really mattered to her.

A minute later Radiance reacted to me. The look on her face—she was curiously drawn to me. There was nothing subtle or real about it. There was a frigid presence about her, clearly unnatural, and it was powerful.

"I've heard about you." She looked straight at me. "You are a very good friend of some of my very good friends."

That took me by surprise, I didn't have any friends. It was bullshit. Her known trademark—sullenness became secondary, overcome by this unexpected energetic assault. Later on, I would understand it was melancholy and weird sex. She sat holding her hand out. It felt predictably cold. Making me feel uncomfortable, like I wanted to take a bath. Behind me Muriel was doing her utmost to maintain her dignity. No one was speaking to her even though she was by far the prettiest woman in the room.

The quiet was getting uncomfortable, I didn't know what to say. Finally, Magritte grabbed at the void, striking up some chatter with Muriel about her modeling career, the difficulties of working in winter clothes during the summer in Central Park. There was a question about the first time she ever did a nude shot for a photographer, who then tried unsuccessfully to fuck her. Everyone's concentration was on the pending answer and that visibly bothered Radiance. The two of us commanded attention, probably because we flatly appeared as outsiders.

Radiance made it apparent she wasn't going to stop.

"Brane, it's coming back to me . . . you're a great friend of Blake's . . . as a matter of fact, he's been telling me about a case you worked on. An extraordinary fight about an inheritance."

I didn't answer. There was a look of uncertainty about her like a chipped glass you might be able to drink from and she almost began to drift but something kept her on the subject.

"Every time I have lunch with him, he speaks of you; how he loves your work, your legal stories. He comes to your country place and rides with you, seems to adore you, absolutely."

"Adore me?" Blake's case was minor, but I discussed material subjects with him. However, he never set foot in my country house except once and he never mounted Blackhall or Whitehall. I questioned her rap. Total exaggeration! Goddamn fatuous! I can't stand people who speak in unfounded facts, chunks of them like fishy salmon canapés at a bad opening.

She was still seated, in that distinct manner acquired by a refined upbringing. It glues the ass to the chair and keeps the spinal cord erect as a floor lamp. The rapidity of her tongue movement amazed me, flapping, and flicking nervously but inaccurately.

I never thought anyone knew about Blake's insignificant estate case or that he pretended he rode my horses. But some of the things I was doing were known in a very small circle—guests who had stayed at my house for the weekend and had experienced my odd manners; I ignored their presence even though I'd invited them. Although I said I hated legal work, I had to do a lot of it then and I must have shot my big mouth off. Whatever problem was current usually occupied me more than the people I had around. So, I spent hours in the dining room clacking away on the keyboard composing briefs, laughing to myself while I was suffering through the tedium of legal work. Sometimes a guest who knew nothing about the law would walk into the room and ask me what I was doing. It happened that particular time I was working on a matter which Blake, in that short visit, found exciting and evidently had talked about to Radiance. It came back to me that I talked way too much around Blake.

I cracked a small smile. It curiously felt painful. At the same time, I thought about why I wasn't looking straight at her and was aware that Muriel's eyes were fixed on Radiance and me. Some guy and his wife were staring at me, forcing me to shift my attention back to Muriel. Everyone was listening to the conversation, weren't they? A spark between us flashed, twisted wildly around the room, getting everyone's attention. She was the flint and I was rubbing against her.

Finally, I replied, "Oh, I know, an art case, the one involving a Pissarro that they claimed was a Nazi looted painting," was my clipped quick sign of intelligence, since everything seemed to have been said for me. The inner lawyer was telling me to keep my big mouth closed. Anyway, Radiance went right on without any prompting.

"Being an attorney . . . that must be positively fascinating! I don't know how you have time for all of it. What type of law? I mean, do you specialize in art? Criminal, divorce?" She must have said the same thing to a thousand lawyers over a thousand coffee tables and she sounded as if she had been around for a thousand years.

The standard questions again, but this time I wasn't perturbed. I wanted to give her precise answers. Not the kind I gave Muriel, answers which most of the time had no connection to what she'd asked me. Now that I look back at it, I was struck by such pressing curiosity and that her interest seemed fully ingenuous. But strangely at the same time I felt as if I were speaking to a naïve child who could learn something from me. Yes, Radiance would profit, understand the vital, obscure facts of life that took me so long to learn. So, I started another speech, and I was full of them, but this one wasn't as nutty as my Biata kitchen monologue.

"I do trial work, mostly . . . you know, go to the courthouse, hang around the hallways waiting for my case to be called. Half my time is spent waiting. Then I get inside court and do an act in front of a judge or a jury. Walk around there as if it were my own living room." Then I was suddenly alone, ranting quietly in my head; I could barely think, saying to myself "What the f am I doing? She already knows all of this."

The room and the guests were distant and out of synch, then my voice burst out loud as if the volume gain control was cranked,

"I act like a madman, using some old saying I made up that the jury thinks they've heard somewhere, sometime when it made great sense.

That's how I win." I closed my lips.

"I mean get the client a win." I laughed under my breath and went on full of anxiety. The bitch was having a bad effect on me.

"But I'm not always in court. I do quite a bit of work on the phone; my head is made out of black plastic. I sit in my office, feet on my antique desk, rattling words, just words, packing them into legalisms that will make my opponents settle before we ever get to court." The rap made me push through the horror I was feeling as if she had control and was manipulating me.

Now Muriel stood listening, watching Radiance's reaction, becoming overtly jealous. Like a sunburn, I could feel her anger on my back. The game of backgammon had long been abandoned by Radiance. Her opponent wasn't interested in my rap and was playing both sides of the game. Purposely, Radiance had freed herself to irritate Muriel, swiveling her attention back and forth between Muriel and me, keeping the superficial ball of conversation in the air, playing with us, her toys.

"So, Brane you must have tried hundreds of cases, exciting cases; did you ever try a murder case?" This was getting stale.

"No, I never have but I'd love to."

"Well, what would you do . . . that is, if you knew your client was guilty? Would you still represent him? What are you supposed to do?"

Though I'd never come close to trying a murder case and I despised criminal law, I'd always responded to that cliché in the past. It'd come up only ten thousand times, but now I was going to be skillful—teach the inquisitor.

Just before I launched into my prepackaged rap, I recalled another time when I'd seen Radiance. It was a year ago. She was actually with the same crowd the first time I'd seen her: the downtown art minions and social butterflies. That night she'd sauntered by my table wearing tight-fitting blue jeans and high, spiked heels. Although her legs weren't very long, she created the illusion they were. She had that androgynous swelter—both sexes intensely competing.

I thought about that night; I gave her a thorough appraisal, trying to determine whether I was attracted to her. There were just two imaginary photos of Radiance: One I was snapping, the other I was pulling out of a desk drawer and staring at to see if I recognized the subject. Yes, I admit that ass of hers caught my attention a long time ago, but so did thousands of other asses that I forgot as they moved past me on the sidewalk. And I don't remember being excited when she appeared then. I didn't say to myself or to anyone else "there goes...who the hell was that?" No, she wasn't like Terry, who could provoke a man to rip her clothes off or to kill himself over her. All of that was in the air.

As a matter of fact, I said then I was never going to be out of control over Radiance. Probably because she was so wanton I couldn't keep up with her. Suddenly I felt better, maybe in control of, at least, myself. But at the same time she appeared lost, helpless. She was going nowhere—a fumbler, now making these feeble efforts to keep the screenplay running between her and me, a total stranger. Yet I was going along with this comedy, intrigued but again truthfully not really attracted to her.

Then everything seemed distorted, and I couldn't get a clear picture. She was too soured, pale from what looked like drugs. More precisely, gaunt. It seemed she'd never taken proper care of herself. The way her black hair was weirdly done up: every other strand combed, leaving the odd-numbered ones kinked. Her bleeding-heart-shaped mouth had too many teeth. No tits. Another flat-chested wonder. But from the waist down she was memorable.

I had to break off this this self-conscious parlor game. The first image of Radiance was affecting me. It made me sad because I could see that she was pathetic. But something else was wrong. All wrong—I was confused because I wanted to walk away from Radiance, turn to Muriel, take her by the hand and go on with the boredom. Radiance was a pest—her questions were a weak punch against nothing. No, goddamnit, I wasn't going to tolerate the Muriel situation either. No compromises. Thank God the thought came into my head, that I had more than two choices. Muriel would be phased out soon enough. The slate wiped clean. I could start all over again, maybe I'd be fortunate enough to not find myself in the same situation. This pattern kept repeating itself. No, I'd break it, fill this cherished life with worthwhile experiences and people who would contribute something. At the same time, the smallest poke at me would've caused a lifetime supply of insecurity to burst like the Hindenburg.

I never answered Radiance's question and instead I turned and asked Muriel, "Do you want something to drink?" For the moment I played the gentleman.

"Yes," she said sharply, unable to suppress her anger.

I looked to Radiance and to Muriel—like a pitcher checking the runner on first and then turning to the batter.

"Excuse me, I'll answer that question later," I said and went to clear my head.

As I reached the bar, Franco came downstairs, accompanied by an Italian couple. Franco introduced me like a steamy plate of mussels, "Here's the lawyer!"

Larry was one of the two men who were sitting in the living room. Mistakenly, I thought he was European, but he was just American with a Euro twist. Lots of those in NYC. He was older than everyone else, plump but not fat, graying at the temples. One could bet he was as well-groomed at six in the morning as he was at six in the evening—a man in uniform—a pinstriped suit, a Hermes necktie, shined brown oxfords. Larry was right, right, right—right school, right club, right people, all those rights made a wrong. He was fifty, inherited a huge fortune, spent his life in the sun, nursing a cinnamon skin color, compliments of Palm Beach and Long Island. With his wealth, he bought a new set of friends he'd trade in every year when the new model showed their faces on the society page. Every time he opened his mouth it was an invitation to leave the room.

Larry was painfully loquacious—in the worst way —everything he said was irrelevant. He needed attention.

Biata said, "Larry was very funny and entertaining during the first six months of our relationship, since I didn't speak a word of English. I thought he was so different because of the way people reacted to him."

We were seated at the dinner table. Twelve of us. Larry sat between Magritte and Muriel. Franco was directing while Larry was acting like a dilettante, grinding esoteric facts into Muriel's ear.

My eyes were tracking Radiance while she made her mind up—which chair would capture that fantastic ass. It was a matter of pride, that incredible bottom was her way of meeting the world. The Marvin Gaye song, "Let's get it on" was ringing in my ears. Make it stop, no that was impossible.

The interrogation went on from appetizer to the last after-dinner cigarette was snuffed. Radiance asked a million questions and I answered every one like I was a game show guest. We covered one another in bullshit, confirming what everyone was thinking—we were one small step closer to sleeping with one another. That didn't occur to me.

The guests were amused, but Muriel wasn't. She clearly saw that I'd given Radiance too much attention that rightfully should have been showered on her. The group was blatantly conscious of Radiance's come-on and equally insensitive to Muriel's displacement. Each pair of eyes irritatingly spot lit me, then Radiance, last to Muriel, synthesizing the mini-drama. Ironically, Radiance's questions were progressively more ignorant and so was I for responding like a donkey led by a trail horse.

For after-dinner openers Radiance asked, "How would you bring up a child?" Knowing she was on maternal ground that would irk the shit out of Muriel or any woman for that matter. I replied, smiling in a way which I thought would have me established as a masterful family man conversationalist.

"Like beautiful plants, just water them . . . nothing more. Don't try to influence them to do anything, especially don't try to model them after yourself." I wasn't serious but Radiance took it to heart, though it was clear that Radiance would never dream of having kids.

The remark brought laughter from everyone. I wanted that—to throw a roadblock into the social dinner talk. But Radiance couldn't be stopped.

"And Brane, do you feel the same way about manners, that they just arrive one day when you don't have them? That they're organically grown?" It was a reference to my barely middle-class background.

She leaned forward, asking the question pompously while I thought about important things that an intelligent person might've asked. A dead-serious expression froze on her face; again I responded to her derisively, although I should have kept my mouth shut.

"Manners . . . you must mean things like table manners?"

"Yes, that's a good start."

"You must mean training a child to obediently maneuver forks and knives and to sit still at dinner.

"I wouldn't want to raise a tyrant with perfect table manners."

"That's not the point, absolutely not the point, you lawyers have the facility to make everyone . . . everything sound silly," Radiance snapped. Nobody agreed but she went on.

"What if . . ." She thought for a moment. Her head shaking, like an Indian butler, she said, "Your child is invited to Buckingham Palace. Don't you think it would be pretty damned important then?"

I rubbed my ear. Maybe I wasn't hearing well. I looked at Muriel for some semblance of good old common sense but she was boiling inside the stripes of restraint. The rest of the diners waited for the volley to continue and I just shook my head. Enough. Radiance and I remained in the living room after everyone had trickled around and Marvin Gaye was still serenading.

We were alone. For about a half hour, Radiance and I talked. There were an infinite number of topics to which she knew the questions. When the conversation waned momentarily, I went to the john and she wandered into the library. Returning, I sat next to Muriel in front of the fire, trying to compensate for an entire night of ignoring her. In the presence of strangers she was a master of composure and she appeared to be unflustered, having a fake good time.

The record on the turntable was fading. I started to say goodnight to everyone, shaking hands, perambulating, being told the standard "I'll call you." Only Radiance stayed out of the picture, sitting in front of the fireplace, her back to the rest of us. Maybe she was cold, certainly her personality was icy. Before we left, she shifted her head slightly and managed to say, "Good night." Nothing more. I was receiving another clue of attraction, me to her. No that wasn't happening.

Franco and Magritte hurriedly walked us to the door, helped us on with our coats. It was cold outside but the night was clear, beautiful, the moon was full and it was after eleven o'clock.

"Why don't you come by for lunch tomorrow? We've had such a lovely evening," Magritte asked, with Franco agreeing behind her.

"I'm going to cook," he added, then changed his mind. "Or maybe we'll drive back early if you don't come."

Before I could answer, Muriel was tugging at my coat, pulling down on the pocket. She wasn't up for another round in this ring.

I paid no attention to Muriel. Magritte was intently waiting for a reply; her eyes widening in a strange way, staring through the two of us. It was if she knew that Muriel didn't like her and Franco. That look made me uncomfortable, I didn't feel like myself.

"Yes, that'll be great," I replied. Muriel was disregarded.

Once I said OK, I realized some very funny things were going on in Franco's and Magritte's heads. They were trying to keep Radiance and me in the same place at the same time. Was there a conspiracy between the three of them? They were setting me up with Radiance? No, that wouldn't work, it was too far-fetched. I decided I'd avoid Radiance. I wasn't interested and that eliminated the pressure I felt from Magritte and Franco.

CHAPTER IV

The drive home was funereal now that we were off the social grid. Only a few words were said. "Change the station" and "Light my cigarette." I took the back way over very rough country roads, which had been gutted by the fall rains. But the full moon lit the road up as if were lined with street lights. The little sports car fought its way in and out of each crater, a perfect metaphor of the state of our relationship. By the time we were home, she'd sighed every known form of exasperation. I wasn't going to deal with it. I went straight to bed, fell asleep, although the sound of a howling dog kept me up, but while I was half awake I didn't make the faintest move to console her.

The party, Radiance, none of it was important to me except I felt deeply lonely, stuck in this senseless quandary. Nothing was meaningful. It was tiring to keep on meeting people, to repeat myself to myself in a desperate attempt to find the solution. Whatever was keeping me from suicide was wafer thin. This was the third-in-a-row, post-summer sickness I was miraculously living through, fighting to stay painfully alive. Every day by noon I'd have a migraine that lasted until I went to bed. It was impossible to work. My head hurt so intensely I'd ask clients to repeat themselves many times and they must have thought "Man, this lawyer is dumb." I pushed myself through it, going against a blizzard, forcing myself to study each sentence to see, to understand when or how it happened. To force myself not to take it seriously was the only way out; everything could simply be reduced to units of days-weeks-months that I could check off on a calendar and be made to pass. The end would always be quick and inevitable.

The next day, Muriel and I awoke about eleven o'clock. The sun was so strong that I felt I had to run away from it. Now came the horror of daily existence: I couldn't stand being awake and was afraid to sleep.

Silently we dressed. We went into separate bathrooms. We came out and had a robotic breakfast, I letting her handle all the conversation any way she wanted. Now I can't even recall what she was talking about, but I do remember pretending I was in Rome, sitting at an outdoor café looking at the street's cobblestones, drinking espresso with a pretty, eighteen-year-old girl, brown hair down to her ass, who could not find a cheap place to live. I listened intently to her problem, drawing on my cigarette. There was nothing I could do for her except take her back to the hotel.

When I concluded, arbitrarily, that breakfast was over, I went into the dining room and worked on the sixth draft of a difficult memorandum of law while she retreated to another part of the house where she couldn't be accused of disturbing me. Around one-thirty I finished typing. Without consulting her I climbed the jade-green carpeted stairs to the bedroom to change for late lunch at Magritte's. The possibilities of what could happen that afternoon did not occur to me until kimono-clad Muriel appeared in the doorway, staring at me like a cop passively watching a crime being committed.

"I don't want to go . . . go along without me." She said it not as a possibility for her to tag along, but as a decision she'd made. She was trying to make me feel guilty. And I was supposed to agree with her—I should go on without her, carrying with me the guilty sting throughout the lunch. It was a relief to know I'd be leaving any second, that I'd be over at Magritte's free of craning my neck around to look at her or thinking I had to check to see if she were all right. No question, Muriel must have thought I wanted to press on with Radiance to see where it would go. I didn't. My twisted mind was made up that she was just too weird. Seeing my friends again and taking a break from work were the only thoughts I had, other than putting distance between Muriel and me for the rest of the afternoon. I had to get out but when I started the car I was overcome by anxiety, my mind was overwhelmed and I began to spin out of control, or was it the car going down the road sideways?

There I was slipping right down Violet Avenue getting close to the Hotel Randolphe, hoping Room Thirty-one would be clean, the bed made. If they tucked me in they would charge extra because they charge for every little goddamn morsel. Then suddenly I was there in my room, thinking too much about my life. How could I live in a place like this? Humanity is dislocated, I'm always trapped in confined spaces—a room to eat, to wash, to excrete, to sleep. My apartment or my house produces that effect on a larger scale, I get smaller all the time. I want endless freedom, no forms, so I can make a formless scream.

Let's call it a day. No, I don't pour a drink and punch on the television. The first thing I do is sleep off the day in the late afternoon. When I awake, about 9 p.m., I read. Yes, that's correct. Books are to be read, not just collected, usually in sets of four. Don't worry, the other three will have their day. When one begins to interest me the other three patiently wait under the bed, like friends I used to have. You have already noticed I don't have any real ones of those.

Very seldom do I go out of this hotel. In the old days, I was out all the time. The museum at night for parties and openings of everything— restaurants, movies, plays. I would clip a black tie on and go out.

I didn't like to move because I hate making sounds. The tenant below will complain about ceiling noise, report me to Hans. Since it's unlikely I'll be going anywhere for a while, I have to keep active. The time in the world, time, time, time, that fucking commodity is the only thing, thing, thing. I'm not taking advantage of it. Guilt, for the sake of my nonexistent offspring, for posterity I should shake things up, let them be devoid of anything negative in my legacy. For the uncaring world I must produce something so I won't be forgotten. My tenure, left in their life behind.

Right now, I can't work; I'll have to read my book. Later I'll go down to the hotel library, it's full of yellowing paperbacks that tell you how to saw, sew, make furniture, dance the cha-cha, travel in style, strip furniture, eat well in Europe, and fix television sets. I can't stand people who write about what to do with time. How to manipulate time is a full-time activity labeled life.

Today I didn't wash, I was allowed to order room service. A cheeseburger, vanilla milkshake and onion rings—all delivered on a tray. The food here is damn good and they also have a gourmet menu, first class. As for laundry, no gripes, it is very efficient—I can't stand dried sweat. There isn't a day that passes that I don't get out of my clothes, but it didn't occur to me to take them off right yet.

My hands are feeling scabby. There is a pattern to uncleanliness, around the hands, the mouth, moist forehead, ears constantly dirty, the feet, under the arms, the fingernails. Dirty hands and unwashed hair. Dirt splattered on me from everything I touch.

The sun is finally going down. The blank sky is the first good thing that happened today. No fucking clouds. Tabula rasa. What a rotten day—glass shards in the eggs, damp coffee grinds on the kitchen floor from elbowing the percolator. That stinking hot drink got onto my pants, gray flannels, my favorite. The dry cleaner down the road near the pharmacy and I will have to negotiate this one-time fee. The shoes are probably ruined as well. Coffee with its indelible grime stains the imagination, then travels through the body's freeways.

Now let the sun shimmy down to my feet so I don't have to consider slipping into another "nice day."

Damn, I am glad there is sun.

I only want to see outside at night, but the hotel windows are filmy. They don't really like to clean around here. Next trip to the store I'll purchase Windex and paper towels and show them. I never open the windows unless the weather is cool. When it is hot, keep them closed and that's a hotel rule. No win.

This morning I stood upright after I woke. Today like every day I stretch, tell myself I feel like shit and shut off the alarm. Then every day I step on the tile floor of the bathroom and stare at the mirror. I look like a lump of shit. So, I try to wash it away by getting into the shower. While the water runs over my body, I am persuaded I am becoming a new man, retrieving my, reworking my, researching my, re-creating my, rejuvenating my youth. I can't find my rebirth in the shower. Goddamnit. Where did it go, I ask my ass? My wrinkling, and wrinkled ass, will never be rejuvenated. Stretch marks like an old YMCA geezer.

Shit! I plan, on the spot, a new exercise program that takes twenty minutes a day. In the morning is when. My stomach feels like the roof of a Quonset hut. The only time I lose weight is when I have emotional problems. Women I can't forget. The pain goes straight for the stomach. Although I feel terrible, I look great, except for the expression on my face. So instead of everyone, all the long-term residents in the hotel tell me I look terrific; they even ask me why I've lost so much weight. "What's wrong?" Fuck them, too.

After the shower, my clothes for the day are to be selected. The same clothes that the hotel supplies including that robe that ties in the back. There ought to be one thing to wear for all of us—a canvas coat with plaid epaulets, enormous silver patch-pockets and rubber boots sewn onto the hem. Instead, I have to debate myself about velvet pants and a white sweater. How am I going to cover my body? Jeans? But they are made for kids. So what? I have reorganized my looks since I awoke and now, I am convinced I can fit the same pattern of an eighteen-year-old.

So, I am dressed at last. I ambulate into the kitchen. "Boil water" is my command. Other hotel guests, call them "residents," are doing the same. Coffee, sugar, milk. Drink it.

The right hand reaches for the briefcase against the wall, and two legs carry me to a steel door. The always-obedient index finger stabs the button. The box in the shaft lowers me to the ground floor. Tony, the little hotel bellman, tips his hat. Before nine in the morning, every day, he's drunk. Sometimes he wears two neckties and I think I am seeing things. I really like Tony. He died a few weeks ago. The life of the lawyer moves on.

I have left the hotel. I hail a cab. Then I sit back for twenty minutes in dense traffic, quietly inhaling carbon monoxide, gassing up, worrying about all the work I have to do.

Now I recall Friday. I wasn't in the hotel, rather I was in front of the entrance to the building where my office is located. I fished through the pockets of my coat and pants trying to remember where I put my money. I only had a twenty. I scanned the façade of the building and remembered how much they've raised the rent in the past ten years I've been a tenant. No time to review the lease, the man is sitting there looking for the fare. The driver's waited patiently while I got change for that twenty I finally found from the concession in the lobby.

My office is on the seven. The elevator stopped on each floor, driving me insane. Finally, I am on my way, down the terrazzo corridor to the office.

All of the old lawyers, real estate brokers and accountants are in the men's room taking their morning grumpies. The over-seventy crones. From nine to eleven, the hallway reeks of their antiquated dung fumes. Someday it'll be me and that year's cynic will be thinking about me pushing the key into the john door.

I spent another stock day inside the office or was it the hotel, feet on desk, phone in ear, cigarette in mouth (sixty times a day), coffee cup in hand? Three cups of light coffee enter the body along with the twelve scoops of white sugar, eight affidavits, three contracts, five conferences during which I perform "live advice" and at last it begins to get dark. Another day passes that I didn't have to work construction. I turned the lamp on, and the color of the light made me think "How the hell did I ever get into this routine?" My time is passing. I lied to myself that I am not caught. On its own, my head shook back and forth as if it belongs to what I used to be.

By this time, the pocket watch I used for a clock (it's cradled in the folded arms of an ivory, meditating, male, Chinese sculpture which sits on the right corner of my desk) said eight-thirty. Dinner with or without a companion? I thought about it. What will it be? Last night's salad updated, last year's conversation streamlined, then fish, steak, dead bird, dead animals all over the table. No, I was going to lunch at Magritte's and I was getting the fuck out of The Randolphe Hotel.

It had turned out to be one of those gray Sundays which threatened to rain and spray cold, misty air. I drove through the bad weather, my mind made up I would not show any excitement over Radiance. I also faked my mood, feigning I was listless, implacable, blasé. While I drove, I thought I am the one who is unaffected by the outside world and I was out of the restraint of the hotel. Apathy is warm, snug, insulating but a lie. It makes one attractive, doped-up looking. For example, it magnetized Muriel, brought on Radiance, but it also made me as blunt as a liar's smile. I said to myself, "Women like the absence of uniqueness in a man. They want white shirts and politeness."

Apathy played by these rules brings you to the attention of the "non-caring elite."

Now after the drive over the same bad roads with my crazy thoughts, out of the hotel and away from Muriel, I entered Magritte's house and I didn't give a goddamn about anything. Across the living room, once again, there was Radiance reading or pretending to read a clothbound novel, author Sartre. Or was she just playing hide-and-seek? Way the fuck over my head. The spine was turned out, advertising her fake intellect to those who bothered to look. That was my ultimate conclusion. The book slides to her lap; she smiles. She has too many teeth and the tip of her nose grows so close to her lips she could touch it with her tongue. Oh God, what the f am I doing here?

In my mind, I reaffirm she is not my type, not attractive enough and too eager. It all confuses me, but I am drawn to this thing and move forward, closer, stumbling, tripping like I am trying to find a light switch in a pitch-black room. We were not alone. Everyone else was in the house, but upstairs, in the kitchen or coming from or going to things like tennis, volleyball.

"Hi . . . Radiance." The right inflection in my voice emphasized that apathy was hard at work. "What are you reading?" I asked the sucker's question. Damn hypocrisy!

A new game of conversation started, beginning with the list of her proof that she is not the idle rich, but the typical, well-read, idle rich—Kafka, Sartre, Styron, existential all the way back when . . . even Nathaniel West, Thomas Wolfe, Thomas Mann and other Thomases. We had many things in common—the literature we'd both read in the vector of our vacuums. Yes, how we, the indolent, killed the time waiting for life to turn its ignition. But all of the truths are disguised, wrapped in black blankets, as we tried to recollect the passages and the chapters which were so remarkable when we read them and exclaimed, "Oh, yes, damnit, isn't it just like that?"

During all of this, I was watching her, the way she sighs, how her head moves away from people. Her elegant hands, the bitten painted fingernails. She's in deep pain. Her white sweater is stained, she apparently can't smile. Juxtaposed was Biata—perfect, fastidious and mature but that didn't hold my attention.

Suddenly, Radiance stood, spun around, and walked back and forth in front of the fireplace. The blaze and roar suited her and the show unlike that lawyer who pitched selling in North Carolina. It was still foggy outside.

"The Green Leaves of Summer" was on the stereo plus the moist air that Sunday afternoon was curiously haunting. At the moment, I rationalized wildly, irrationally that I was going to be friends with her, whatever that meant.

A guilty picture flashed through my mind—I imagined Muriel was actually back home, in the bedroom, watching a three o'clock Cary Grant Fifties color film, "North by Northwest," wondering how the hell she got into this predicament, why wasn't she in the film as Eva Marie Saint instead of some dumb female waiting for a jerk like me. The rain splashed on the patio behind and I began to feel uncomfortably cold so I moved toward the fire and Radiance. Although I didn't say anything, that was a bad move because she walked out of the room.

After lunch, Magritte, Biata, Franco, and some hand-picked Italians returned to the living room. I twisted sections of the *Times* Business section and fed them to the fading fire. The scent of uneasiness sat in every corner of the room. They watched me, they watched her while she and I stared at the ceiling over the sound of hissing wet wood. I couldn't take it, so I turned to Radiance and said, "Let's go outside, a walk," finally dropping the remote possibility of something between us. I could've taken her back to my hotel room but there wasn't time. That would freak her out for sure.

She moved away from me, surprised I'd asked and then she nervously laughed, checking everyone's reaction, and said yes.

We walked down the driveway, over to a yellow meadow, talking animatedly as if we were finding out all sorts of interesting facts about one another. I looked down at our leather shoes that were getting very wet, becoming concerned she'd use that as a pretext to return to the house. Part of a white pine corral fence was in front of us. The upper rail had fallen out of its slot and it lay at a forty-five-degree angle across the lower rung. Don't ask why I stopped to repair it. Then I felt her heavy eyes on my back. She was observing my walk, my shirt, how my pants fit my ass, the Euro places I'd probably traveled and anything else that might make me "social."

"Don't do that!" she cried anxiously. "This place is too perfect; it needs a few defects, things that are wrong with it that will never be fixed." Suddenly, I felt a deep chill from the winter wind, but it wasn't that cold or windy.

"You're right," I agreed without thinking, except I remembered a friend of mine in law school who had a girlfriend with a scarred chin. He used to tell me how no one or thing could be beautiful without a flaw. Flaws and laws.

I damn well knew flaws are important, especially to women who have them. Anyway, it was another move between us that had me doing what she ostensibly desired, but I knew she was unsure of herself. "Maybe the fence should be put straight," was going through that head as the right thing to do. She reminded me of a confused child who appreciated the beauty of a rose seconds before being pricked by the flower's thorns.

As we stood there, she began to tell me something and stopped. I asked her what she was getting at, and she answered with a question: "Do you see me ... with a man in a suit?"

"Very much so," I replied, being facetious. "A plainclothes cop."

"How's that shirt doing for you?" She stared sarcastically at my chest.

"My Ralph Lauren shirt, I just bought it, I liked the fit."

"Is the man on the horse a friend of yours?"

"No, we haven't met yet, he's usually galloping on a Polo field."

She wasn't acknowledging my sense of humor and vice versa.

"But there is a man in my life, I always think of him dressed in an elegant Italian suit. And I always see him at the end of our relationship; he tells me that he doesn't want me, that it isn't another woman, but that he can't be committed."

I listened because there was going to be more information—the same type I had heard from other women in the beginning. Then it all sounds fascinating. Then there was that damn chill. It felt like it was coming directly from her.

"For more than a year I've been involved with him; crazy, I can't get that image out of my mind—I see him in a suit. But he's not like that. He's German. . . you won't believe this . . . but he looks just like a buckaroo. Cowboys have been a fantasy of mine since I was a child, having one as a boyfriend, dreaming about riding off on horseback with him, country music playing in the background. Waking up in the morning and his black boots are under my bed, his guitar is against the wall.

I made a wisecrack about immigrants in ten-gallon hats checking into a dude ranch, which she disregarded. Her story was hilarious, but she was intense, excessively serious.

"He's German. You ought to see him in cowboy boots and a football jersey." I pictured Hitler in snakeskin boots, wearing an orange University of Texas football shirt, addressing the throngs at Nuremberg.

Hitler was a freak for the Wild West. A German writer named Karl May wrote a slew of westerns although he'd never been west of Berlin. There were Wild West clubs in Germany then and now. So, I should have cooled my sarcasm and let her go on about the cowboy *sprechening* in a drawl, rustling up grub, holding a pot of coffee, tying up his horse in the livery, feeding it *wiener schnitzel mit bratkartoffeln.*

I nearly exploded with laughter at that point; what stopped me was her perplexed face. The scene was completely foolish—her jabbering away, me listening, telling myself to be somber, attentive like she was one of my crazy, paying clients. Then the story was not so humorous. It was probably intentional when suddenly the subject of her father came up. The rain intensified, she blinked, closed her eyes for a moment and I no longer thought of her as a garrulous, intellectual lightweight.

"This man in the suit . . . in ways he's like my father. I was born in France." She was waiting to see if I was listening. Her father was dead by her tone of voice and I already knew all about him.

"My father put France on the map . . . did everything, captain of the Olympic ski team when he was eighteen, flew a piper cub through the Tuileries and under a bridge near Notre Dame, every day he was in the papers for something he did that was spectacular. And every night he was in a club— the best clubs—the movie starlets, stars, drinking and dancing while all of them watched him." She pronounced "them" like the rest of the world was just a lump of black shit.

There was a silence while she looked for my reaction. What could I say to that? It was shallow and unimpressive, so I didn't say anything, remarking to myself that there must be more to this and I knew it.

"And when he died, he was one of the highest-ranking racing car drivers in the world. He accomplished all of that before he was twenty-five, can you imagine it? Yes, the man in the suit, he reminds me of him because . . . I don't know why I am telling you this because I hate him. I hate him for what he is doing to me, and I hate my goddamned father for what he did to my mother, destroyed her, me and my sister. He never spent any time with us, just those whores, but I know he loved my mother and I know this man loves me."

This was the basic poor-little-rich-girl saga. Her head unnaturally rolled to the side as if she didn't want to be seen crying.

"Don't ask me how I know he loves me (she was talking about the cowboy, I first assumed); it is something I know about (maybe she was talking about her father). It didn't matter since she felt the same way about both of them. Then she acted as if I didn't understand her, as if she's said too much for me to comprehend. In fact, I hadn't bought the story. The whole thing was uncomfortable to hear, way too insane. But I didn't walk away. I didn't feel like leaving her even though I was soaking wet.

"When he was twenty-nine, he was killed. I wish you could see his picture. He was dark, handsome, strong, and probably the world's biggest playboy. Yes, that's what he was! Everyone encouraged him to race, except my mother, my poor mother. What she must have gone through because no one would listen to her! That's because she was American. She hated all of them, my father's family, friends, and they hated her as well."

Then she paused for a second and said, "Tell me about yourself, Brane." That was some fucking ego abandonment switch.

Raindrops were pelting my face. I peered at her through the corner of my eye. Her head was bowed, she was stuffing her knuckles into the front pockets of her narrow-legged jeans. I used the long silence to look at some of the fall I'd missed being in the city—leaves dropping from a copper beech tree, swirling through a windy whirlpool. My mind spinning, trying to understand why the f I was here.

Every time I'm with a woman for the first time, her life story came up as if it had been printed like an amount due on an invoice. Not just women but humans of any type or gender have a vast capacity for repetition. This woman was different but so much unlike me—words trotting out of her mouth, hopping over country fences, down the driveway through living rooms. The comedies, tragedies, while those hands of hers went into her pockets, her hips and just flailed out of frustration. Won't it go on forever just that way? I asked myself, but I ignored all warning signs and just kept my car on the tracks as the train approached.

I talked, now it was my designated turn. Even though I knew she was crazy as could be, certainly not as crazy as I was in this fucking hotel, but she underscored the desultory pattern of my end of the conversation. I told her I understood because that's what listeners always say. A side of me humored her and another side of me humored me. Just insanity, but I didn't know that either. Moiety, thousands of them, splinters, halves of thoughts, halves of flashes, half-beings and personalities. Everything a pro and a con and nothing made sense except I was getting an urge.

I was silent now and thought about laying a monologue on her just to see how deep her craziness went but I slipped down Violet Avenue right into my room and maybe she heard me say "Next stop, Violet Avenue"?

I am naked now. I took my shirt off last week. My left shoulder shivers from the cold or it moves around nervously from a chill I always seem to have. Usually, I try to exercise to get rid of it. Games, shit I haven't played chess, checkers in so damn long. I'd like to play Monopoly for money but I can't find a willing adult. It's been years since I have been motivated. I've had no interest in sports, games.

"All athletes are bums," is what my father said. He was right. That soured all my interest in recreation. The last time I picked up a tennis racquet it made me feel like a criminal. Well, if Dad knew how I felt now, he would have gone to the sporting goods shop and bought me a pair of cleats or a baseball bat just to keep me out of trouble. There was no whistling in the hotel, and I couldn't wash the car or chew gum on the Sabbath. I wonder what he'd do if he saw me like this, madman, nude next to a pile of blood-stained clothes on the Sabbath. The result was my father's fault for not liking Mickey Mantle or Joe DiMaggio or just a tiny bit of baseball. I am just acting out a well-written script, hand-fed.

See, I did all this—see these photos. That's me copying life. That's me making my first long-distance phone call; that's me wearing a suit for the first time; and that's Dad and me at the Empire State Building. He's holding me out over the metal barrier on the 108th floor, telling me to look down. What the hell have I done now, conjuring up all these memories? I need a drink. A bottle of whiskey. If I were drunk, I wouldn't have done it (what?), but I could have laid it off on the booze—the state of intoxication, not the regularity, the normality of sobriety.

But I held it all back and said nothing to the best of my recollection.

"Tell me about yourself, Brane?" repeating the question, "Didn't you hear me?" I was coming out of my Violet Avenue fog. Wasn't that how she started me off or did I do this to myself? It wouldn't have been the first time.

"Cut the shit," I said to myself, looking away in disgust but hiding my expression from her. I felt like I was sliding down the side of a porcelain wall. At that point I couldn't go on, couldn't take the best and the worst of my life and lay it all out in a showcase for her to glare at. But she didn't quit.

"You make me so interested, Brane," God, it sounded so awful, "... turn around ... I want to look at you." Yes, then I turned toward the fake flattery.

"It is so incredible, you've done so much . . . a litigator, a well-known lawyer, and you are so reticent. Downbeat. Maybe it frustrates me. I've never done anything; for years it's been like that except I have studied acting. This is the truth; I am a very good actress!" So is every woman I have ever met. I held that in check.

Her sudden assertiveness following the lack of confidence went through me like an ice pick. Where were we, on page 10 of "The Importance of Being Earnest," vacillating between country and city personalities. Now I was in a position to tell anyone what a screwball chick this one was, but I would tolerate her totally. Again, she wanted to talk, talk and talk.

"Yes, that's right! The one thing I know — I am a great actress." This time it came out like a question and the corners of her mouth were raised with the uncertainty of a theater curtain responding to polite, short-lived applause. It made her teeth look unusually white and very sharp. Then I felt sorry for her, again telling myself she was just another sad case.

There were many things I could've said but I chose to be quiet. Purposely, I wanted to see her suffering, the full extent of it. I knew she needed something from me, and I was going to make her ask for it. Day after day, Muriel was asking for the same thing, and I'd never given it to her. But with Radiance it was different. Eventually, I would give that to her or maybe not.

The weather was getting worse. I could see she was cold and I was freezing, wet and any second she'd want to get back into the house. It was foolish for me not to take the initiative and say, "C'mon, let's go back inside." Instead, I waited for her to decide because I didn't know if I should just invite her up to Room thirty-one. Nervously, she stared at that fence, then at the ground and went on.

"Damnit, I am a great actress. It is just that I can't go down to those horrid theaters, standing in cattle lines, auditioning. I am not like everyone else, and I shouldn't be treated that way. Besides, I just want to do films. Theater isn't at all what I am after."

"Was there anything to say to her dark red lips?" I questioned myself. I didn't want her to resent me for meddling and I didn't want to counsel anyone. I knew myself—how quickly I can create the father image which can destroy sex. At that point I was thinking of sleeping with her but I wasn't feeling anything like an urge. She was incredibly ugly, but I couldn't stop looking at her, those oxblood lips. I think I made the decision that it was something which had to be done, that all this talk was just fuck language and she went through it with every guy she met. And wound up fucking them the moment the words stopped.

She asked, boldly, "What about you? You were supposed to give me your life story, come out with it." She was reading me, becoming cute, momentarily smiling, and turning her waist back and forth like a five-year-old.

Against all of my principles I calculated, structures of what I was going to say. My head whittled a few expressions full of innuendo, then articulated a facile witticism and went into the conversation, responding to her as if she had asked the most sensitive but answerable question about my past life.

"Where should I start . . . I have so many answers for the, that question. But I want to be honest, I want to say to you . . . to what, I don't know!" I pretended to be stable but I was jittery because in the moment I was on Violet Avenue. "To know about . . . me." That sounded all right. I was gaining every bit of her interest, it seemed to me, but like most people she'd probably listen to a yelping dog with equal intensity.

"To understand, that I was brought up differently. In a tenement above a grocery store on a street called Violet Avenue." How did that slip out, she'll think I'm nuts?

"Actually, I am dignifying the place. It was a slum, a warehouse for my father's grocery store. That's probably why I get sick whenever I go down to

SoHo and listen to those assholes talk about how great it is to live in a factory space, remodeled to look like an apartment!"

I checked her reaction. It was sympathetic. At the same time, I felt pity for her, watching her hand pressed against the tear-drenched wrinkled lace collar. It reminded me of the thrift shop clothes some of the customers wore in the store. That helped me through another childhood sense I had about the rich being so goddamn separate from the poor.

"Since he was five, my father was working in the store. Even before he was five, he used to walk my grandfather, who was blind, to the place every day. That was my grandmother's fourth husband. My mother's family came over from the Ukraine, my father's from Vilna, Russia, around 1900 and opened this store I am telling you about . . . selling something that doesn't exist anymore: Penny candy. The store was about as big as a parking space."

My voice became tremulous, as I was sensing that the story was way too much for the circumstances. I was coming across too heavy, too impoverished with a shitty background, too violet.

The rain was really pouring down, but I kept on speaking through it, trying to see how long I could hold her attention—not long. She backed up after the words "penny candy" and gave the sky a fast look. Those words would make any rich person turn back. Good thing I didn't tell her my dad's favorite movie was *Pennies from Heaven*.

"Let's go back to the house," she interrupted. "We can't stand here!" That made me feel like all the other times I've been asked a question by someone I knew who would grimace before I answered.

Of course, she was right about the rain. It embarrassed me since I wasn't successful in holding her attention. The grocery store versus the racing car driver. I was angry at myself for giving her an opportunity to tell me what to do. Now I had to follow her to the house or insist, like an ass, that we keep chattering in the storm. There was no time to decide. She was five steps up the drive. I ran and caught up. She turned.

"Brane, I really like you." Her arm came to me. My defenses went down, and I slipped hers through mine, without answering her. The smile on her face said it. She knew the game was well underway, that she was in the lead, but she had no idea about Violet Avenue. It's a game changer. Then she asked if I would show her and her friend the road back to the city. She'd get ready. I agreed, wanting to spend more time with her but that was out of the question.

After she went into the house I walked to my car, pretended to do something important like examine the New York State registration in the glove compartment. Then I read the inspection sticker inside the windshield over and over until they came out. They pulled alongside, then I glanced at Radiance, who seemed to be laughing at me. I paid no attention and started the engine. All the way to the road I watched them in the rearview mirror; I knew they had to be discussing me. Then at the Saw Mill Parkway's entrance I left them with a fading wave, thinking that the entire afternoon was a non-event, that I'd totally exaggerated the weekend because of the flatness of life with Muriel. As I headed to the house, I began to sink, remembering I had to return home with Muriel.

CHAPTER V

We were back at my house.

"Did you have a nice time tonight?" Her voice was complaining and curious at the same time.

"It was all right. Did you?" No, I wouldn't go into any detail. The color of the day—Sunday faded white was really depressing me at that moment. Twenty minutes before, the grayness, the rain had been exciting. Radiance had distracted me from being down. Together we had eluded and ignored the drizzle, I told myself, forgetting momentarily how she wanted to go back to the house. I thought wistfully that had we taken advantage of the rain, gone to bed with it like we were in a small flat in a New York City brownstone on a Saturday afternoon, we could have made love, the rapture of the water dripping onto the air conditioner, the bedroom windows fogging from our body heat. I tried to contain myself, avoided looking at Muriel, but she had her own ideas of control.

I stood next to the bed and just stared. The quilt began to rustle; I knew it was being pushed away. Out of the corner of my eye, I watched a nude hip roll toward me. There was a time when I worshipped that move. For some reason, I don't know why, I sat on the edge of the bed. Bored with the hip, the thigh, the ass, the legs of Muriel, I tried to not look at any of it as it circled around in front of me. Then Muriel, the total package, was next to me, cuddling.

"Honey, I want . . . to talk to you." Her breath was my breath, she was too close. Slowly, I moved my shoulders back, acted, faked there was nothing wrong and that I was going to listen to her, but only if she were going to speak about something innocuous—the weather, television, some old dinner we ate.

So, I said, "Great, what do you want to discuss? It is a miserable day, isn't it?" She didn't reply. "I hate it when it rains."

Whatever I said wasn't going to matter. She was on the track to laying her cards on the table.

"I want to know . . ." She hesitated for a second, "How you feel . . . I care so much for you . . . when we are together, I have such wonderful times. Things like yesterday can be worked out. Everything will be fine." There was that smile I liked, and her long thin hand played with her hair.

Again, I made a note, jotting down how pretty she was, but my emotions ignored her. Where was Radiance? My mind was running out to the parkway. . . . Radiance, where the hell are you? Yes, I can picture you, probably lighting a cigarette, crossing your legs, smoothing the nape of your neck, chatting with your friend about the weekend, me, the goddamn German with those blood red lips.

Then I thought I was hungry and didn't give a damn about Muriel, about what she was saying. And was there anything I could say that'd make her feel good? The seconds passed, revealing by silence the answer for her—it was all a waste. Pockets of tears formed in the corners of her eyes while my hands went to my forehead. The parkway was again settling in my head. I could see Radiance digging into her handbag to answer her cellphone. Dinner plans are confirmed. Then she glances at her watch thinking about Sunday night. The simple pictures, the dumb scene, amazed me. What was I going to do? What was I doing with Muriel, listening to her, pretending to be alive, a symbol of a female, while I stole thirty glimpses of someone else who I said I didn't care about?

The edge of the quilt fell away from Muriel's legs; she was naked from the waist down. The only hair she had on her body was between her legs. I looked at her nudeness, the olive tan, the carved shape of her ass, callipygian—the perfect magazine ass, the movie star ass, the fashion show ass. Impeccably shaped legs. I hated being there.

I hated myself for all of it. The schism in my reaction went right up the middle of my insanity. And while I disregarded Muriel's needs and considered only Radiance's, my own well-being finished last. None of these ideas were quite clear to me then but now I know myself better. Now I know things are never clear—one assumes the task of resolve, carrying the possible solutions all the way to the grave.

So, I didn't sit there empty-headed, waiting for it to all pass. I tried to work out some approach, but that proved impossible. She spread her legs, scissored me around the waist and pushed her lips against mine. The tears flowed, zigzagged down her cheeks across the fine, pen line that indented her chin.

I couldn't make love to her again. At that wicked moment I had to tell her it was finished, just the way I had been told by so many women. A porcupine crawled around the inside of my chest; I was not adept at such things. Would an observer believe that I wasn't just another shallow, over-endowed bastard, who thinks he has the world by the balls but chooses to be stereotypically cynical? That's incorrect and that's a perfect assessment of the New York City jabber. Muriel simply wanted someone that didn't want her. She said to me: "Honey, please go down on me . . . please, you know how much I like that!" The tears, legs and arms wrapped 'round me like a python. "SHIT!" in dripping red neon exploded in my head.

This demand of hers was worse than the client who never pays me a dime and insists that I start an antitrust action against Apple. She wasn't kidding; she tried to force herself down my esophagus. She was never really kidding about anything; she was one of those people who have no sense of humor. They don't know what's funny or what isn't. These people know nothing. Truly they are a perplexed group. God knows how they survive, other than being the unconscious sycophants—the go-down-on-me users.

If it had been Terry telling me to get onto that pussy or if it were the first night with Muriel, I wouldn't have been able to stop myself. Muriel, the goddamn audacity! Here I am on the edge of letting her know I have no more feeling for her than a waiting room magazine and she's telling me to stick my head between her legs.

Then she said it again and again, throwing her head back like Venus in repose, expectantly, like it was already happening. Pulling my shoulders in, undoing myself from the clasp of a soon-to-be-ex-lover's grip, I said, "Please! Muriel, what I want to tell you . . . "

"Later!" Her arm went over my shoulder, tighter around my neck.

"Please! Stop it. I am going to tell you this!" I was insisting. My arms braced around my knees.

Every form of behavior, every ounce of strength she had which would stop the ineluctable words which were on the tip of my tongue, she mustered. Tears now as thick as raspberry jam came from her eyelids while I yelled, "I can't go on with this anymore. . . . It isn't right for you, fair to either of us." My voice broke into pieces.

"After the last few months, you know I have been terrible to you." My voice finally professionally composing itself, "You should be with someone who will be sweet to you. You're too good to be kicked around like this."

Every cliché sped out of my paradoxical, inconsiderate mouth. After all this time running over her with a mental tractor, I was being nice. The time to be kind is when the door is being shut for the last time.

The first time I went out with Muriel I knew it. But my system wouldn't permit me to tell her so until she was thoroughly involved. Back then I needed a beautiful body next to me. Now in this hotel I can't tell who the hell is beautiful. Her bawling came, much harder than I anticipated, like a child who fell off a tricycle onto a concrete sidewalk. Her eyeshadow morphed, her reddened face swirling into black and white surfaces while her body was painfully naked, not the usual beautiful nude but now sexless, helpless.

"You motherfucker, you're a bastard," I said to myself, forgetting again what Terry and the others had done to me that put me here in Room Thirty-one. Whatever happened to my convictions? Self-preservation took over. The past taught me nothing.

The covers were pulled over her, so I knew at least she'd shelved the cunnilingus. But she was crying. How long can someone sob? I waited and experienced a good amount of pain. No one gets off cheap; I wound up feeling worse than her. When I was a kid and saw someone throwing up, I'd laugh at first, then I'd throw up.

So, there wasn't anything to do except wait, and listen to her. She talked through part of it.

"Honey (again honey), I know you don't mean what you said." Her wrist wiped the soggy eyeshadow in a straight line to her chin while her voice stuttered through a plea:

"We can . . ."

"We can what?" I asked stupidly.

"Work out all of these problems, have something beautiful in the end. Everything takes so much time. You must try to be understanding. Both of us are so worthwhile and we are so right for one another."

Finally, she seemed to be finished. Then it was my turn. I couldn't stop myself; words come so fast.

"I don't feel disposed to twenty years of hard labor in an emotional jail while you feel like you're in the sun all with our kids who everyone says look like you, or me, or the two of us. Work what out? That I hate the relationship, hate the eggs-in-the-morning—they taste like ball bearings. Your accent makes me feel like I am negotiating a pound of salmon. Every drop of red and white wine I drank with you I want to vacuum back into the bottle; yes, that's it—reverse all of it, make you feel the way you did the second before you laid eyes on me. Why? Because I don't want to hurt you. So, you lose but then I'll be next. Someone is out there, waiting, stalking the invisible, who'll break my cold heart. And you'll hear all about it during lunch in a sidewalk café, while you're telling your new boyfriend that 'we were just good friends'!"

The density of this outpouring of one stupidity after another was incredible. How can I be so carefully callous, thick-skinned for the sake of what? And if I turn to you, Muriel, and say something like "This isn't easy," would that make you, ultimately, hate me less? No. At this point check the manual—the best thing to do is shut my mouth because it will get worse. The more I say, the kinder I am, oh shit! It'll give you the rest of the insecurities—those that make you watch the clock, hope the phone is going to ring. No, and no again. It isn't going to be me. It isn't the things you said or didn't say. It was just you—the metaphysics of the little computer in control which is making you love me and me hate you.

The curtains, the lacquered bookcases, the poems, the bambino we're not going to have, the long conversations on a phone with your best friend about you, talks with my best friend about me, and all of those talks I had with nearly everyone about how I was going to get out of this relationship with you. The wordiness of it all, the goddamn words stumbling through each page and paragraph of the times I didn't feel like speaking because my mind was white from existence. The main reasons I stayed with you so long was you kept promising me we'd go to bed with various of your beautiful friends. But you never came through.

One night in the beginning of "us" she explained a scene she had in Paris and once in Rome. She went to a nightclub, apparently with the same old boyfriend. In these types of clubs, the waitresses fuck the customers during dinner. It takes place right at the table in front of the other patrons. The background music is lowered. There is an extra charge for that.

As the story goes, Muriel was starting on the foie gras when the waitress with the Las Vegas showgirl body approached Muriel and told her "To turn around." Muriel licked her lips, she's instantly hot, her face flushed. Then she turned around, her dress is unzipped, the kiss on Muriel's back, that kiss moves to Muriel's lips. Muriel taken by storm; she couldn't resist as her date watches the encounter; he had carefully set this in motion that afternoon by phone, ordering a performance. Muriel hated making love to a woman, but pleasing him was far more important.

"I'm naked on the floor with her. He is watching, smoking." I can imagine the rest, he turns to snort a line of coke. The waitress is pushing her tongue inside Muriel who is saying "Kiss me, oh kiss me." Muriel is trying to please him.

"My Christ," I had said out loud while I was listening to Muriel's mouth, hoping this would be the basis of our relationship. Muriel continued with the story: "We are rolling on the floor; I am now on top of her. She tells me she does this every night of the week, it's her job, but that we are so natural as lovers. Then he pushed me away and took the waitress from behind. I went to a corner and masturbated. The customers were watching but acting not very interested. The food is very good and that is why everyone goes there."

That story is what kept Muriel and I together for so long. Without that narrative, I would have broken the cold news to her long ago. Clearly, I am rotten through and through or else I was just trying to get even with Terry. Muriel never came across, never found any such women for us. She said, whenever the subject came up, "I saw one today, but I didn't have a chance to get her name." So maybe she was lying all the time. But I doubt it, because she always sounded so damn sincere. One afternoon, she came to my office after it was all over and said she had found someone.

"Brane, I have this voluptuous African friend, model, she is a lesbian, but she will go to bed with us." However, that afternoon I was too removed from her to seriously consider it, though the illusion of what could have happened was so appealing to me. The illusion of fucking that which one cannot fuck, or is not fucking, or that one will not fuck. All the different types of fucks. My head jerks when I think about Muriel because I wouldn't mind fucking her right now or looking forward to it tonight.

Anyway, I asked her, "Muriel, please stop crying?" Nothing affects me more than the sound of a woman crying; my mother always got to me that way.

She interrupted me, "You think I cannot get over you! You're just like every man I know—weak!" The tears stopped. "Just because someone cares, you find yourself so incapable of accepting it. I am sick of all of that. I don't have to say, 'What the hell is going here?' I know!"

Watching her was a beautiful experience. This creature bemoaning her fate, the unevenness of it. Surely, she could step outside and find someone else in a minute. Surely in my fucked-up world. The contrast of the heiress committing suicide over the auto mechanic, the king over the seamstress, the stories of unevenness—I hate all of them. I hate humility and hate when beauty and power succumb to righteousness, to reality.

The hysteria was over. Some final words, just words warbled through the wetness of catharsis. I answered her again.

"I wish I knew, I wish I knew. Believe me, Muriel, I would tell you because I don't want to see you suffer or anyone else for that matter. There is no explanation."

Again, I was probably lying. I didn't give a goddamn about her fate or anyone else's. I just wanted out, easily.

Strangely, those were the last words spoken about the end.

During this bleakness I had a bath, dressed more or less for the Sunday night drive back into the city. The fancy cloth suitcase of Muriel's was packed with the silk underwear, the French skin cream, the French perfume, for the last time. Why it upset me, I will never know. Every time I walk down Violet Avenue, I ask myself that.

CHAPTER VI

Will I ever get the hell out of this hotel? Will I ever retrieve my old energy? Will I ever get married? If I touch the curtains to push them aside, to see what is going on in this world, they'll probably fall apart. This room frightens me, makes me afraid to move. And I don't have too anyway. . . . I can sit here for the rest of my life. The room phone is disconnected. I won't pay the bill. No one will speak to me. Shit, I speak only through a pencil when I write. The pencil sharpener, where is it? Yes, later I'll record some of these thoughts.

Now it is later. I made a note of that. Yesterday, I believe, there was a noise in the kitchen . . . sounded like a rat scrambling across the floor to the cabinet under the sink, probably after a jar of bread crumbs I left there when I tried to dry out a fresh fish. I hope it is a rat, at least I won't feel so all alone. My forehead is my only companion; I must have stroked it (as if it were a dog or cat) 500 times since I woke up.

This hotel provokes me but I am not staying there now, I have to finish with Muriel. I even imaged Muriel was up here a long time ago. We watched a film together and ate rolled grape leaves, Virginia ham. She told me, "Brane, your philosophy is Danish. . . . You are like me and my friends in Denmark, who are like characters in a book." What a waste of time it was for her to lie to me.

We began to leave the house. My back was starting to bother me, fucking sciatica. It must have been the same injury from the springtime. Every type of agony seemed to have been growing inside me. The first days of October are here again, Muriel and I are in the car on the parkway, racing to the city through the twisted green, yellow, and red autumn proscenium.

Muriel fixes her lip gloss. She stares at the center of the windshield blankly. I am not idle. I rotate my neck, rolling the pain in my back, using the axis of my spinal column. This is our last hour together; I exercise for what is coming next. We are going sixty, as uncomfortable with each other as a mongoose and snake. But we are side-by-side, trapped in a metal box. The only thing I can focus on is the leather sleeve which covers the steering wheel, my leather gloves changing from one grip to another. One cigarette leaves her lips, another is lit. Another exit passes and out of habit we glance at one another every few minutes. I know she was convincing herself to never see me again, to hate me; she wasn't succeeding.

About forty-five minutes later we drove over the bridge near the Cloisters, crossing the Hudson. Again, I was injected with the romance of time flying, the sun falling through its own rays riding on the river's wrinkles, bearing down on my wrinkles. How many Sundays in the same light, with the same feelings for all those who came before Muriel? No! I was matriculating at the Academy of Relating Myself to Love. Then, as I came to all of these wonderful conclusions, she learned over, her left shoulder into my right, her left hand on my right testicle. Locked into another grip. I began to twitch. What the hell is this? I thought things were complete, done.

"Honey," damnit there it is again, "I want you to go home and think about, think over what you said to me. I know you don't mean it."

The last few words she whispered in my ear were like a crepe being shuffled off a spatula. An SUV full of kids making faces passed us in the outside lane. The corner of my lip rolled between my teeth. I bit down hard, abusing myself for not sending her back on the train. Several minutes passed, she didn't release her hold and didn't complain.

"Now I want you to get a good night's sleep and not to think about me. I'll be all right, then you and I will meet for dinner later this week." Her hand squeezed my left ball and a large smile broke out across her face. She was talking to herself. I was thinking to myself. There were four of us traveling together.

"I am going home!" I exclaimed, trying to dispel all of her ideas.

"And I am not going to be able to see you for dinner this week."

Her finger ran along the inseam of my pants' leg. Suddenly, she pulled away, looked out the windshield again—that blank stare. She stayed like that until we were in front of her apartment house. I got out of the car, each one of my steps feeling the hard pavement on the Avenue. I came around, releasing her into her L-shaped apartment.

It pained me to pull her suitcases out of the trunk, to watch her say hello to the doorman. The one who'd seen a thousand guys like me ask to ring her apartment. Then the morning comes, and the lover boy leaves and the doorman says "Good morning," knowing that 23D got fucked last night, that lover boy is wearing yesterday's socks, shirt, pants, feelings.

Muriel, I remember when I saw you through your white cotton slacks, could see the outline of your ass, the lace trimming on your underwear. I was drinking a glass of white wine and I said to myself, "More than anything I want to go to bed with you! I want to fuck that!"

Now she is going through the lobby, taking a right turn out of my life. I am ambivalent, regretful, but I know it is going to pass. I am tricked by her absence. "Come back, baby, come back," I started to say, but then it was replaced by "Fuck it."

I returned to the car and started to experience rebirth. I was on my way to the hotel, right up Violet Avenue. Is it true that I am free of her, no more appointments with Muriel? My head cleared from the eyebrows backward like a bedsheet. I flipped the radio to a music station and I was ready for the upcoming romance. But then I reconsidered, there is nothing; I am finished with all the dinners, phone calls, discussions, dressing and undressing, gesticulation, coitus, and questions. Take a look in here, that's my insides. A hologram of scars, imprinted on my stomach lining, crisscrossed swords, tracks from excessive ice skating on the sensitive pond of my soul. I have been bombed, hallmarked. The savagery of alienation. But I know that—can't return, can't go back. The periphery is behind me, there is no division. Everything has been taken care of; now I am a ticket holder, allowed to watch the show. No one can explain what is happening. It is not allowed.

After I went around the block twenty times, like a wandering Jew, I found a parking space and went further up Violet Avenue to the hotel. No one was around to celebrate the end of Muriel. I turned the television on and off. Nothing but a jar of mustard and a bag of potato chips was in the fridge. I read a shitty novel. I played a record. The book and one side of the record— they are both made for repetition. The book is thrown to the floor, and I punched the amplifier's power button. Breaking up with Muriel yielded no relief in the first thirty minutes.

"Let's see what happens," I told myself. I wait. Gabriel's horn is not blowing. How did I get in this tight spot where I don't want to stay awake and I don't want to sleep? Of course, I couldn't endure much of that mood so I went out, back to the delicatessen on Violet Avenue, where I can't buy light bulbs and toothpaste. The night clerk and his pal are always there, permanent as weather.

Next, I eat a salami sandwich, drink a Coca-Cola, stand momentarily in front of the museum watching two fourteen-year-old boys, who surely go to a private day school, pitch street rocks at Calder's stationary twenty-foot mobile growing out of the Whitney's moat. They laugh, the mobile's defenseless steel members ring, resound, move slightly from the attack. The boys become frightened and run to Park Avenue, home to their toy-packed rooms. There was almost a full moon; I slid my hands into the back pockets of my pants and walked further into the night. An old movie actress walked by, smothering a has-been writer with after-dinner kisses; her head turns because she knows me. I am her husband's lawyer. What do I care? I have me to think about, but I can't think and turn from her. I won't tell her husband.

On the sidewalk, suddenly, I was invaded, trespassed. A man appeared in my mind holding up a placard. It read "Radiance Tempest"; it made me laugh and shake my head, crookedly, from side to side. I unsnapped the next two buttons on my shirt, felt my chest as if I were trying to soothe an erstwhile pain.

"She comes across like a dumb ass, she's unattractive, ugly in fact, affected and I am pleased that she likes me," I reported to myself. The sandwich was finished but I was still hungry. Nothing unusual about that; I never satisfy my needs. I walk in the street starving, or wanting to get laid, but not calling any one of those phone numbers, wanting to sleep but staying up all night, attending women who hurt me when I am seeking affection. The list of my deeds of self-denial is endless.

I returned to my room, not famished. The door shut behind me as I put on the foyer light. There was a possibility I'd run into Radiance on Thursday night—Magritte was having a party—and I knew she'd be invited. The hungrier I became the more I thought of her. I wanted to call her, but as long as the party was on, I could take the chance and see her then. For the past hour I'd been thinking about her. I grabbed a lock of hair in my left hand and ran my fingers through it—one of the better expressions of concentration I've perfected. But nothing was really going on in my mind except the excitement of Radiance surrounded by canyons of boredom.

I took my pants off and sat down on the bed in my usual spot in the Hotel Randolphe room. The boredom overtook me, made me angry that all I had to do was go to some delicatessen, see some movie star in the street, watch those idiotic kids passing me in the SUV. There was nothing to do, so I went to sleep, but I woke up almost instantly because I was being attacked by a gorilla with stainless steel arms. It brought me right out of the enemy territory—the unconscious. I wanted to sleep again but I could not. I would not. I had to see all of this happen that night—there was no escape. Sleep would've drowned me with monstrosities pummeling me; staying awake I could fight them. Where did it go? My being that kept me out of jams like these. Robbed, I was robbed by the death success breeds, the plateau where one is made to be identical with everyone else—free plastic surgery. My insides were ripped out, machinery replaced them. Me, I, that gorilla took over, with its iron arms and legs. Before I was a hairy bastard, until the lawyer, that asshole, took over. The first thing he made me do was lose my sexuality—the savagery of being alive. Then I let the system wrap itself around me. I became the man who could never go out because his plants were dependent upon him. They had to be watered. So, I was brought this close to death but not permitted to die. Honestly, if I had known, I would have preferred the sanctity of ignorance. But I am to blame for all the years spent developing the brain, the business acumen, so I could be become a businessman. Now the brain is like one of those peculiar children—a boy with long, bony legs, a slight potbelly, long arms, his fingertips touch his kneecaps when he stands up straight. He wears glasses with round frames, has freckles, red hair, and a high forehead. This kid studies all the time and people don't want to talk to him because he's too serious. I want him and my brain to cut the shit. My real persona wants to come forward, but I am too immersed and the voice through which I can communicate is muffled but not silenced. Maybe I'm dead because the only sound I can make is on paper.

Monday, Tuesday, and Wednesday went by slowly. Each one was a study in the body's desperate yet natural needs—there wasn't a faint craving for Muriel's presence but there was the growing immediacy, a deep thirst for contact with Radiance. It was stronger than anything I had felt since I was a teenager. At work on Monday, about three o'clock, my cell phone rang.

"I just hung up with Radiance." Blake. His voice was like a schoolboy's teasing a classmate. "She is wild about you . . . thinks you are great."

"Is that why you called?"

"No, I wanted to say hello after I heard you were carousing in the country. You never invite me."

"Really, I should one day." I stopped there because I knew better with Blake, that I should wait because Radiance would be the inevitable subject, he was eager to spill the beans. But he didn't as we waded through the silence. Finally, I continued because I'm often stupid when I should be clever.

"Haven't heard anything about Radiance, your friend. The feeling I had was she's never very subtle, she practically devoured me with questions. The woman has an infant's curiosity for information, wouldn't say knowledge. It is hard to believe she's twenty-five."

"I agree."

"What is it then, about her? I think the whole thing was a misunderstanding," I tried to blunt the point of the conversation.

"From my point of view, I think she's a good girl to keep as a friend. You know her family is very rich, possibly one of the richest in Europe."

"That I didn't know, and for some reason I don't believe it's important. Like I said I think my meeting her was just another of life's misunderstandings, we have nothing in common."

"Brane, you're too goddamn dubious. I'm not going to argue with you about that and it doesn't matter. You'll never see any of that money."

"I don't want any of it and I don't know what to do with that kind of money."

When it came to women, Blake's number one consideration was wealth. Once he told me that if he were going to put up with all the shit women dish out, they might as well be rich. He was real Upper East Side philosopher. In his head, Radiance passed all the social tests, his basis for judging her as a friend. Never underestimate the power of status and wealth. If you don't have it, you'll never be accepted by the people you don't like.

"You may not want any of it, but you just may have something there. My opinion is she could be a great girl in the right man's hands. We go back quite a way. Nothing ever happened between us. I have known her for years. Most of her time she spends alone, never fucks just anyone. In that way she is a strange bird. If she talked to you that much you must have been really pouring it on." Blake was now eagerly doing all the talking.

"I wouldn't call ours a long conversation.

This conversation is quite a breach of trust but let me tell you—she's wild about you. It is worrying her very much that, she's pissed off that you haven't called already."

"I don't even have her number."

"Neither do I. To me it's ridiculous since her number isn't listed and, when she calls me, she even asked, 'How's Brane going to call me, how is he going to get my number?' That's her, though, angry already that you haven't called, interested in you because you didn't call and disappointed because you don't have her number."

There was a pronounced silence during which I didn't allow myself to fall for any of it. The deadly excitement from Blake was all bullshit. He wanted me to ask for the number but the more he spoke, the more I realized he was closer to her then I thought. He must have been around her as a walker or they'd had a mental affair confused as friendship.

The intercom buzzed. Someone was waiting for me. Before I answered my secretary, I told Blake I had someone on the other line, which took him by surprise. I would call him later that afternoon or around the end of the week. The tactic was formulated—let it all slide, knowing that it would build into intrigue. There was to be no call back to Blake, no soliciting her phone number.

At that point I was not playing a conscious game as much as I wanted the passage of time to clarify my confusion and the sensation that I was being yanked in her direction. But on the other hand, I thought she was full of inanities, uncorrectable ones. More importantly than anything else, I found her more hideously ugly—a female Dracula. It was not a consideration that the press described her as extraordinary, enchanting, beautiful, stunning.

So many different ideas were coursing, like river rapids, through me that I was enjoying the confusion, the experience. Not one moment with Muriel did I feel like this. Out of the starting gate I had a substantial lead—being pursued and feeling, what I thought was, disinterest.

"The little bitch isn't going to get what she wants," I'd told myself more than once since I left her on Sunday. There was a challenge and it was me challenging myself not having any idea of what was pulling me toward Radiance. It wasn't as strong as those Southern blow jobs, and speaking of Terry I called her when the Radiance stuff was getting to me this week.

"Brane, I told you I'm a happily married woman, I live in the woods and work at the university. My husband is a wonderful man who is a professor so please leave me alone."

I said nothing.

There was a long pause and then Terry claimed, "Your memories are not mine and we do come up to New York City to visit museums and take in Broadway shows once a month." There was the old prick-tease.

"Why haven't you called me? I could take you and your husband out for dinner." That was rhetorical. Just wanted to touch base for old times' sake. I know we ended badly, but I think about you often and we had something that you can never duplicate. Except I met someone recently that reminds me of you." That should've put the jealousy screw in her.

"That's nice, I don't think she can ever duplicate what I did to you." Very quickly I tried to filled in my defensive blanks. The phone cut off at that same old juncture, and when I called back she wasn't answering. That's life.

Two women too much. Besides, I was tied up with my law practice. I should have told Terry how busy I was. Every day I wouldn't leave work until nine or ten at night. When I'd get home, I'd go through a thick file of complex papers while I ate dinner alone. What a life!

When I finished speaking to Blake, I put her out of my mind. There were several important things to do that afternoon. A new libel case came rolling through the door concerning the subject of freedom of the press, and two guys were my four o'clock meeting. They wanted me to research the possibilities of turning Yankee Stadium into a gay disco during the Yankee away games. The paid me twenty-five grand to contact the club owners and to do preliminary zoning work. One of them kept rubbing his cock and licking his lips throughout the conference. I didn't increase the retainer for that free bit.

I said to myself, "What the hell, I am getting paid for this, too." Part of what they neglected to tell me in law school. He had an advance case of acne, the kind that drips down the neck, onto the chest. I think he had an orgasm in my office. The breathing served as background noise for his partner's detailed explanations of how they were going to set up a dance floor between first and third with trannies running around like mannequins on the playing field catching imaginary fly balls. The admission would be expensive, the tickets priced like Yankee games with rain checks. Great idea.

While this was going on I thought about the stories I could tell. They didn't amuse me anymore. They each represented nothing but work. All the bullshit about what an interesting or fascinating case is a lie. I got paid for only one thing: results. The clients didn't like it when I lost. Once the retainer was in my pocket, the client didn't want to know another thing until "We've won." The money was a trap. I was a kept man, prisoner to my bank account with the retainers, stuck where I lugged around the client's confidential, contorted problems in my deteriorating, deranged head.

On weekends I took their anxieties and worries on horseback through the lunches on front lawns, through every dive into the swimming pool, through each time I screwed Muriel. There was no difference between me and a dog dragging around a boulder chained to its neck, except the dog didn't have to speak.

About seven-thirty I left the office and stopped to buy a newspaper. Radiance was walking over my brain like an astronaut on the moon. I could see her pacing back and forth in her apartment, talking to herself, her chin indented, wrinkled; she's smiling, suddenly angered, pressing her lips together, snapping her fingers, kicking the couch, smoking one cigarette after another; then there is a pause—nothing happens— suddenly she screams out that I am a son of a bitch. The phone rings. It isn't me. Didn't Blake do his job? That disgusts her, she jams the cigarette into a large porcelain ashtray and tries to be polite to the grocer who is calling to tell her that the delivery boy is on the way. She strolls into the bedroom and picks up a copy of a private club brochure in the Caribbean she was asked to join, thumbs its three pages and discards it, tries to light a cigarette with her Alfred Dunhill lighter but the fucking thing is out of butane.

Her face is flushed, snarl red, and she hits the bed with the side of her small fist. This is all the heiress does—wait for someone to call her and make a date.

The pictures make me laugh. I enjoyed her suffering, her lack of control just like me . . . something the money couldn't buy her out of—the moment. Then I gave myself a warning: What was I doing thinking about her so much if I wasn't interested? I couldn't answer the question except to rationalize I didn't have anything important on my mind. Nothing!

I went home and played around with the libel case. I must have written ten thousand words and rewrote it the same way. Hours later, I realized I was only retyping, but the movement of my hands and the exercise for the mind were good for me. I deceived myself into believing I was in deep thought, keeping myself busy enough to stay balanced on the narrow path of sanity.

About 11 p.m., as I was still trying to cover the work, I took a break and made a call to a friend of mine who I thought for sure knew Radiance. I didn't want to call Magritte. Rachel was socially connected through her family, although her father had cut her out of his will. She moved to New York and presented herself as an oppressed heiress. Of course, I was her lawyer.

She and I became friends after a date. Neither one of us wanted to take it further. To amend her depression, she used me, calling me at three or four in the morning, and I was amenable.

She answered after the first ring.

"Rachel, Brane, can you do something for me?"

"I don't know what that means; don't you say hello?" she asked.

"Not today. Let me get to the point." Since she owed me so many favors, I didn't have to be subtle. "Do you have Radiance's phone number?"

"Why?"

"Don't ask, please"

"OK, I'll take a look—hold on a moment." I was not someone she could say no to.

It took her about ten minutes to find it. I held the phone in my hand and read a few pages about Obersalzberg, one of Hitler's weekend retreats. It was in a book that showed the history of Nazism through pictures taken of the Führer at leisure, Germans acting human.

Rachel picked the phone up.

"Sorry it's taken so long; I couldn't find it in my old contacts. If it's working, don't tell her I gave it to you . . . she's very touchy—well, uptight is a better way of putting it—about anyone having her number, or about anyone handing it out. I never called her."

"Don't worry, I'll be cool about it," I replied, reassuring Rachel I wouldn't reveal my source. The word "cool" calmed her down; it's tranquilizing but not as effective as chill.

I inscribed each number with a black Sharpie but couldn't quite form the numbers properly. Her simple phone number took up too much room—the first act of blackness. There was nothing pretty about it. Each number looked like warped thistles and thorns, together an evil forest.

For a few minutes I stared at the card, entertaining the idea of calling her. Twelve o'clock—the right time to phone, to let her know I was not going to follow a conventional tack of waiting for days. Besides, this was a convenient part of the night for a call. Plan canceled. It was better that she didn't hear from me at all; maybe the party later in the week would be the best way for us to talk and see one another. Then I thought, "What the hell is happening? Why am I going through all this trouble? I'm not interested. This is a stupid game I'm playing with myself."

At that point I was the actor who does not get paid for working, that I was confusing all of my characters, the one who hates women, loves them, underestimates himself, the intellectual who has it figured, the village idiot, the masturbator, the hunchback street vendor, the Adonis, the recluse, the unloved, the bitterly desperate victim of experienced fantasy, the overly tough, the sensitive, the generous and the martyr. I went to sleep with all of them very much alive, calculating Radiance's place in my life that night.

The players arose about 3 a.m., entered the tabernacle of my deepest needs, sat at an oak banquet table and ate my soul. What had happened? How was I so transported from the isle of apathy to the center of emotional reunion? My battered, broke, atrophied feelings were arising, climbing out of their casts, throwing away their crutches, signing out of the asylum. I like it, I hated it. Then the committee adjourned without a decision. A list of doubts was left on the table concerning this bitch Radiance Tempest.

Those fangs were not going to puncture my neck. I couldn't stop thinking her face was so ugly. But I was undeniably feeling, beginning to actually feel for her. My brain squeezed itself, crushed her image, wrung it like a washcloth, tried every form of self-defense to eliminate her. But I was being compelled to get over the self-indulgent self-torture of my permanent ennui, to give myself up to this creature. This was not a gag nor a dream which is forgotten; I was given adequate warning.

The dream of her scrawled inside of me, scratched onto the statuary of us bunched together—life in the thick. So that was how it began, and all humans know the type of beast to whom they are attracted, what sets all the responses toward the macabre target of self-destruction—the ultimate, the only road to happiness.

CHAPTER VII

About eight-thirty the phone woke me. It was Blake. He read The Times every day and had breakfast at Starbucks. He had graduated Harvard, wore scarves in the summer and looked anorexic.

"Brane, did I wake you?" Certainly, he knew the answer, as his intonation was clear—he didn't care, deeper down. It was more important to have company at breakfast. He was feeling blue and whatever I went through the night before didn't count. Normally, I'd just let the phone ring early in the morning. But I usually knew when it was Blake. His ring had that pain-in-the-ass urgency. Blake and I had one thing in common: loneliness flavored with depression. Since I'd moved into his neighborhood, these 8:30 a.m. meetings were a ritual of commiseration, the usual topic was the bittersweet journey through life.

"Uh-huh," I groaned. "Meet for breakfast?"

"Yes, I want to speak to you. But if you can't make it I'll call you later, at the office."

"No, no, that's all right, is it anything important? What did you do last night?" I asked, acting wide awake, ready for conversation.

"I'll tell you when we meet"

"Twenty minutes."

Then I forced myself out of bed, getting into New York City's outside world. Blake hated waiting, so I rushed through a shower, picked up my briefcase, shoved some money into my pocket and flew down the steps onto the sidewalk.

There he was sitting in a rear booth hiding behind a newspaper. After I sat down, I kicked him; The Times's Sports page was pulled off to the side and he smiled in one of his countless moods. This was the down-to-earth one.

The waitress brought me a black coffee. I sipped, returned the cup to the saucer and looked at Blake for the news. He was waiting for some reveal, a new subject, so I was to go first.

"What was so important . . . you said you had something to speak to me about. Shoot!"

"Really, it wasn't anything except last night I had this peculiar experience. I was walking down Madison, going to a movie, and I ran into an old girlfriend of mine, Nancy, and while we're catching up on the corner of Sixty-sixth and Madison, this woman walked by with a great-looking man, a goddamn giant. I rarely have seen anyone dressed like her early in the evening, it was light out, wearing long, black leather gloves, black fur coat and red lipstick. Nancy's face turned white, she was frightened. She said to me, 'That's Radiance Tempest. . . . I can't believe she didn't recognize me. We were friends in school.' Damn if I didn't recognize Radiance as well. Then she started to call after Radiance and stopped right away because a limo pulled over. Radiance and the guy got in with a bunch of freaks dressed in black. Anyway, she's something."

What the fuck was he talking about he told me the other day Radiance was crazy about me and now she doesn't know who Blake is. What the F is this: "We were friends in school?" O.K. I get it no one knows anyone.

"That's my point, I can't tell what who she is," I chimed in and played like I was the whack.

"Anyway, that's why I called you; you brought her up the other day." He didn't answer me appearing like we never talked about Radiance. That seemed like a lie but maybe it wasn't him. He stopped, as he ordinarily would, waiting for my reaction to this information about Radiance, his fingers fumbling with a pink sugar packet. A half-amused, embarrassed look shot across his face. Now he was impatiently killing time tapping a coffee spoon, waiting for an answer. The description was too curious, too exact, and of course, I had to ask, "Are you certain it was her?"

"Yes, I knew her years ago. I went out with her, but I don't think she'd remember. I was twenty-eight and she was around my age, maybe older. You know how I feel about young women. Back then she used to run around quite a bit late at night; she could get away with it because she doesn't work. Anyway, one Sunday I took her for a walk down Fifth Avenue, had a quick lunch with her, a good bottle of red and she dashed off. I was planning on getting her into my bed that afternoon."

"Knew her years ago." What the hell was he talking about? Besides Radiance brought Blake up to me and he said he spoke to her the other day. This was getting very good now.

"Oh, is that all, sex?" I knew Blake better, he wouldn't give up on any woman that easily unless there was a damn good reason and now he was going way off the rails.

"Yes, she knew what was going on even back then and she wrote me a cute note during lunch. It said 'I know what you expect of me but sometimes I don't know myself well enough to decide what to do. I don't want you to regret knowing me. Please understand there could be danger that I am protecting you from. Sorry.'"

He and I looked at each other in a weird way but I didn't say anything; he wanted me to ask him what she meant but I needed him to tell me.

"The whole thing means nothing; she never would see me after that. For years I have seen her growing up in the city and she never says hello, pretends not to recognize me. Seriously, I can tell you since we're friends, I had this crazy crush on that woman and I still want to go to bed with her. Now you're in the picture, or might be, is that right?" This was getting good and strange, now I wasn't even sure he was Blake.

"That's correct, you would never fool around with anyone I'm interested in," I answered. I wasn't really concentrating on anything except an image of Radiance and this supposed new man—the guy in the street. There's always another fact or person in love affairs or infatuation, just when you think you understand the situation.

"You mean prospective...with Radiance, or do you mean potential? Don't get ahead of yourself," Blake corrected me, although now I wasn't sure we were talking about the same woman.

There was no answer for that slamming door. Blake quickly changed the subject. For about ten minutes we talked about business and some legal work. The subject of Radiance was done, expect that now I couldn't get rid of a killer image of her, that supposed guy on Madison and that Blake was mad, mad about Radiance years ago and his story should've fucked me up.

On Thursday, business was slow. There was small money owed to me, on top of the regular sums due from deadbeats I'd serviced years ago who I knew would pay in dribs. Every so often I'd start a collection lawsuit against one of them, wind up getting a default judgment, only to find that they were judgment-proof. That's like foolproof. The only route was to have the marshal go to the judgment debtor's house, to confiscate their worthless furniture or a beat-up car.

So, there were no new cases. The phone wasn't ringing and I was totally caught up with my uninteresting, stale workload.

My secretary, Pat, was off. I sat at her desk and looked at the computer screen. No, I was not to get very far. The door opened. Muriel. Again, how fucking consistent but she was looking beautiful. At this rate I was destined to despise beauty. She was wearing a beige silk blouse, no bra, jeans which shaped her ass into tight little horseshoes. I kept my head down, typing.

"Brane, don't you say hello?" The eyes opened wide, the mouth smiled nervously, and she put her handbag on the desk.

"I haven't heard from you this week, I thought you'd at least call. There's a chance I may be going to South America for work very soon. I didn't want to go without seeing you."

My head turned but I didn't face her.

"That's nice." What a stupid thing to say, but I wasn't going any further. How many times had I been in her position? Shifting my weight from one foot to the other, waiting for some female to turn around, to look at me, surprise the hell out of me and say, "I'm so glad to see you," and mean it. Now this was the end. I closed the screen and stood.

"Let's go into my office," I said quietly and pushed my papers to a corner of the desk. The pain in my back came on and I waved my left arm around like a wing. She started to move away, as if she anticipated getting hit, which never happened. How pitiful! She just didn't have any idea of what I was going to do next.

Behind Muriel, the door to the office flew open, striking her in the right shoulder. She looked down and gripped her side. It was the pen man, an obnoxious, fast-talking, dwarf-like, ballpoint pen salesman I threw out of the office once a month. Before I could open my mouth, he started to pitch me.

"Hey chief, I got a real special for you: twenty-four dozen ballpoints, in every color, six bucks a dozen." A dozen was shoved like a bunch of carrots between Muriel and me, grazing her. I ignored her injury and yelled, "Didn't I tell you to stay the fuck out of here this year?"

But I didn't sound angry. He went on not giving a damn whether he'd hurt her. Pens were stuffed into all of his pants' pockets and his suitcoat. For a second, he glanced at her, then back to me. There was ink all over his hands from showing that his pens were smudge-proof.

"Pretty girl, what's wrong with her? Why is she holding on to her arm like that? Does she want to buy some pens?"

"No . . . I don't think so. You dislocated her shoulder when you barged in here!"

"Tell the young lady I'm sorry," he said quickly and continued to sell me, treating Muriel exactly as I had. That was incredible; I was so sure that he'd give his balls to be with a woman like her.

"You're not a lawyer, are you? I never seen one who looked like you, you got a beard. Shave, you look like a bum. You should wear a suit, too. Where's the lawyer in here?

"Come on, lady, I'll make you a special deal because I hit you with the door."

I rushed in and grabbed him. Muriel broke into tears; a handful of pens were shoved against her wet cheek. I had to do something.

"OK you son of a bitch, get the hell out of here. This time, as usual, you've gone too far. . . . If you don't beat it, I'll take back my check."

"What's the matter with you, boss? I got a right to sell to anybody." Then I pulled him backward out of the office, through the lobby and into the hallway.

"Take your hands off me, let go of my suit, chief, I'll leave. . . . I'm just trying to support my wife. . . . I got two kids in college," he screamed.

When I had sat down at my desk, she'd stopped crying and was laughing.

When I looked at her, I began to think of Radiance again. What the hell was going on? It was as if Muriel was sitting there only to remind me of someone else.

It brought me back years ago when I was staying in an apartment in Paris, listening to music on a late Sunday afternoon. The window was opened to the rear yard. My back had been killing me that entire day; I'd aggravated the usual pain radiating from the line of my crooked vertebrae. About every thirty minutes I'd get up from where I was hunched over writing and go to that window, stretch my back and roll my neck around. Two carrion crows were on a high branch of chestnut tree. It seemed like they perched there all day, just like Muriel and I seated in the office. At that moment, I prayed that she'd just fly away.

"I wanted to see you, nothing else," she said and leaned back in the same chair where clients sat telling me their billable problems. Muriel was uncomfortable and edgy even though she'd added that protective "nothing else."

"When we were in the country last weekend I told you how I felt," my folded hands expressing calm.

"Did you mean it?" She knew better than to ask that low-quality question.

"There's no reason to say everything all over again. This situation between us isn't going to change." My folded hands went in the air and then hammered the desk.

"You are so damn stupid," the Danish accent robbed each word of its power. "You must give us some time. I know the way you are. . . . I can help, it can be wonderful between us. You're too narrow-minded to see it. Oh, men like you . . . are so fucking stubborn!"

"So, if you think I'm that stupid, why do you want to be with me?" I asked, but I didn't give a blade of crabgrass whether she answered. The words increased her discomfort. Several more times she repeated her pitch, while I thought about how unbelievable it was for me to be turning her down.

The first time I saw her was at a party, dancing with some older guy. I was with Blake. I said to him, "If I could just get with Muriel . . . I'd give my right arm."

Then he told me she had put him down a few months before and he stopped trying. I couldn't believe I'd ever get close to a woman like her. When the dance was over, I went straight up to her and yelled over the music.

"If I don't scream, you'll never talk to me. I'm going to chase you day and night until I get you. I am not kidding around, you and I will be together before the week is through!"

She went for it and gave me her phone number. That weekend we went to the country, her jeans were off and she stood in the middle of my bedroom in her beautiful summer tan and her red silk underwear.

Now the realization was striking Muriel that she had no choice but to leave. Tonight was the night. The coldness came from what I wouldn't admit to myself. The party. I was going to see Radiance. The image pulled me out from behind the desk and I laughed uncontrollably out loud. It couldn't be helped; even though I knew it appeared I was laughing in her face.

"So, you're a real bastard; you think all of this is funny?" she said and stood glaring at me.

Instantly, I apologized, explaining to her that I was nervously laughing because it was painful to go through this. Just then a part of me wanted to choose her over Radiance but the other part of me shut it down. How could I have told her that Radiance had me running around in circles?

I think she knew there was about to be someone else; I didn't for a split-second feel anything toward Radiance except dangerous amusement. I had her in my mind—she was a helpless, naïve, neurotic child and it would do her a world of good to be with me. My viewpoint was twisted.

"Brane, I spoke to Charlotte the other day." It was odd she'd bring her up. Charlotte was an extraordinarily beautiful African who was a close friend of Muriel's. We'd gone to dinner several times. I was dying to sleep with her. She was one of those calendar girls, thin, elegant, fantastic breasts. After hesitating a feigned second, I asked, "Oh, what about?"

"You know her boyfriend, the tennis player?"

"Yes, go on."

"Well, she told me a story about how they went to bed with another couple . . . actually, she likes women very much. For some reason we were doing a job together last Monday, for a lingerie ad. When we were getting undressed, she made a remark about my breasts. How much she admired them. I was surprised."

Now I was getting hot, but I restrained myself, feeling that it might be the truth. Or I was being led into a trap? If I went on with the conversation and tried to set up a scene between the three of us, Muriel would go for it; later on, I'd have to break things off again, for the third time. The temptation was fucking captivating, downright mouthwatering. And she waited for me to say "Let's get this party started." Isn't that what I wanted from the time I first brought up the subject of a ménage à trois and she'd told me about the club in Paris?

Then I transacted the morality, ascending the plateau of fairness. What a disgusting way to use her! Poor fucking Muriel, down in the devastation of our relationship, trying for the last time to entice me in a desperate way. The word "desperate" set off a charge in my brain, made me think immediately of Radiance. Everything was clear then. The dream of Muriel and Charlotte, watching them make love to one another, was suddenly converted into something I could resist, like the last glass of champagne that would make me sick.

"That's nice. I have to get back to work."

It didn't affect her the way I thought; she stayed cool and said goodbye. The door closed and I knew she felt like a fool, being refused even with an offer of another woman thrown into the bargain. Without any second thoughts I returned to my law office letters. I must have written five of them to people I can't remember.

About five-thirty I went home, stopping first at the grocery store to buy cigarettes. When I walked inside, it occurred to me to get shaving cream. A little reminder from nowhere since I have a full beard. The symptom was recognizable; I wanted to look good tonight, I would trim my mustache and beard. It was the first of all the details a man starts to remember when a woman is getting to him. I started to figure out what to wear from shoes to shirt to cuff links.

Just as I was leaving the grocery store, I saw Vicki, a girl I had had an odd affair with several years ago. My feelings for her were friendly and warm since we made it at night on Route 27's grassy strip just outside of Amagansett. Passing cars honked and flashed their high beams on my ass rising up and down like an oil derrick. She couldn't have cared less about the traffic. Her sense of liberation wasn't lost on our time when everything and anything can happen.

Vicki didn't want to be hurt and she had a point; none of us do. Following our one-night stand, she was afraid because she'd never been to bed with a man as old as me. I was thirty and she was twenty. Occasionally I'd bump into her at the same places in the city. Inevitably, she'd come by briefly, say she missed me, to call, that she was driven mad by me. Maybe that was the truth. She was complex, but whenever I'd phone, she'd put me off. Almost every time she said she was sleeping or busy so call back, or the line was engaged. I gave up. The years passed, interspersed with our infrequent accidental run-ins where we couldn't talk about anything material. By then I was sufficiently pissed about being knocked around by life and time. Vicki was a woman I forced myself to forget and she made it easy by not seeing me. Nevertheless, there was the kernel, the bud that just needed the mildest form of cultivation. That night she could've stopped me from seeing Radiance and maybe from going down Violet Avenue.

She was wearing a vintage black bowling shirt with Oliphant's Mortuaries on the back and black slacks. Sexy bitch. A smile materialized on her face just as she saw me She rushed over and gave me a wet kiss. Her face was perfect, wide, soft, fleshy nose and lips. Everything about her body was soft, sensuous. Her breasts were right in front of my face. Then and there she and that pair of protruding nipples could've been the savior.

"And what are you doing here . . . Brane? I have tried to call you so many times." She was lying through her teeth.

"You always move, and your office tells me you're in court. Of course, I never," she laughed and smirked, "leave a message."

I knew what was coming, how she loved to say things on the order of almost, knowing exactly where the edge was. I ignored her bullshitting. "How are you?"

"I'm fine, everything is wonderful, but I have to run home and feed the cats. That's what I'm doing here. Do you live in this neighborhood? I thought you'd be living in the country." Always some feeble task that had to take priority, the cats, the fucking mail, the electrician, the broken Wi-Fi.

"For the past year I've been here during the week and on Thursday or Friday I head up to the country," again, I didn't pursue her move. I never told her about my country house. The next thing for me to do was invite her for the weekend so she could say no. I didn't say a word.

"I'd love to come and spend a weekend with you, will you call me?"

That was bullshit. It didn't get a reaction from me; I was too battle weary. She pulled a slip of paper out of her bag of miscellaneous gear and wrote a new cell number down. Hurriedly she planted another of those brand-X wet kisses on my lips and sped into the grocery. For a moment I stayed on the same spot and tried to make this event consistent with my thoughts about Radiance. Vicki was somewhere in there floating around in that goldfish bowl and as things turned out like I said I should've chased after her that night. Last chance to get off the railroad tracks and out of the way of the oncoming train.

The truth! I couldn't be involved with anyone. Violet Avenue . . . that encounter with her sent me right down there to my room.

Rats, did I say rats? There aren't any in sight. It was probably my imagination. Fertile these days, isn't it, my boy? Maybe I should settle down and write some simple poetry. That'll calm me. The poet deep in me. Yes, I am not in this hotel room, I am in a foreign country. No space confinement because I live on the sea. The waves, the ocean, millions of creatures down under, it is not a sandy beach, there are no tourists. I am finally alone. I live in a house on the rocky shore and mountains are tumbling down to my very two feet. Giant boulders heave out of the water, confronting one not unlike hostile humans. They have real faces and the waves crash against them, spraying the salt water like rainfall in the sun's face.

The rocks are not smooth; I take a walk. It is so secluded I remove all of my clothes and take a book of short stories out of my back pocket. My hands reach down and untie my shoes, now I am naked on the edge of the world. Now I am going into the cold sea, and I am going to swim as if I were falling through space. No one else is alive for thousands of miles. The sun again turns down, the day is retiring, and it spreads an orange reflection on the water's surface in a straight rippling line to my toes. The water is so damn cold, but I step in afraid that if I drown now, no one will ever find me. Only a pair of pants, a book, a skeleton key in the pocket and a pair of thin-soled white leather shoes. No trace of the man I was.

But it is you and me, God. Like it was the two of us in that hotel room for so long. You neglected, however, to steal my imagination because I don't say the same thing twice, does the refrain of the Fifth repeat in the *Pastoral's* storm? And I must return to the horror of this room and the blood. Why is it all here? No, I wouldn't touch the shirt! It isn't mine, it's yours. Isn't there any wine in this stinking room? At the very least I could drink myself into an extension of my oh-so-limited, imagination. So, I'll pretend I am drunk. The beach is lovely.

I am out of the water, and although the nightfall is cool enough hot air is left to dry my body. The brain is much desiccated. Go on! I have to push myself, cut myself through the jungle thickness ahead. First, I must visit the beach once more. A walk toward the east, away from the setting sun. The beach suddenly ends and I climb steep rocks and come upon a strange house. The ocean rushes below but there is no place to go; there is no road to the house and its bricks are weather-beaten. The door is locked and the blood-red shutters are closed. I try my skeleton key, but it does not fit. A chest-high doorway is open, and it leads to a thermal bath covered with a concrete pendentive dome with square holes in it. The light peeks in at different angles. The water is warm, and I go in and sit like a Roman emperor in retreat in the south of Italy. This satisfies me. Man needs drink and behind me the monastery sits at the foot of the mountain. It has a wine cellar.

Dear God, I visit the monks. A stream runs by the monastery along a concrete drain turned copper-green from the surrounding moss. Two painted red iron gates are shut. An oblong brick Spanish tiled roof. It is the home of the ascetics, sitting on a knoll behind. The reward denied to those who suffer for the time being; the monks are long gone, in permanent retreat. On the other side, the sea slaps against the rocks. I open the rusty gates. In the wall-enclosed yard there are smooth stone steps descending to the earth's center. Seven steps. I go down without thinking that this is the beginning of hell. No. It's where casks are stored. The floor is drowned in waist-high sea water, but I wade through in the dark, my extended hands find a spigot. My mouth quickly is under it and the rotted wine pours fast, spreads across my face, a furnace blast of sulphur dioxide. Is this the blood in which I am covered?

My room was in about the worst shape I could imagine. Cigarette butts stuffed into broken champagne glasses, I hadn't changed the sheets in weeks, dirty laundry that was celebrating a six-month anniversary on the kitchen floor; I despised that place and everything about it. Someday I will hire a maid and she'll go through it like a real trouper. Even the TV screen had a film of dust two inches thick; I didn't watch that shit anyway. The first thing I did, though, was to try to clean up a bit. Weird, no one was coming over, and no one ever did because I never invited them.

Actually, I began to wash the dishes; they'd been drowning in sink goulash and leftovers. I put the vinyl's back in their jackets. The laundry was collected and thrown into a pillowcase. Still, the joint looked like hell redecorated by the village idiot. The round, coffee table glass was the last thing I'd fix, Windex it. It was clearly a piece of junk, supported by Spanish wrought-iron curved legs like a barrel with half the slats missing. You know who loves the Spanish motif, don't you? The top was so scratched! I made it look like damaged merchandise at a railroad auction. Then I sat down and cleared my throat. The time: 7:45 p.m.

I picked up a piece of cardboard on which I had scribbled all of my recently acquired cellular numbers. I was about to call Blake and interrogate him further about recent Radiance news, just to see where he was at now. Instead, I thought I'd blow her mind (and mine) and call her. Knowing that I had every reason to feel confident; I knew she cared, she had no one else, she was totally lonely, and she respected me.

I became unusually nervous. I dialed 5, 6 and hung up. Maybe, yes, it was better to just run into her at the dinner party. Maybe she wasn't invited and why the hell was I phoning? The plan, what the fuck was the plan, the strategy? There was none. The mind clouded suddenly, the rules of rationality, experience—out the window. Now I was lost. But I picked up the phone and dialed 563-48 and hung up. Progress. I had to pull myself together. Didn't I do that so well the previous weekend? Where did this stupidity come from? For a moment I clasped my forehead just a bit different from the times I was in court trying to get my opening address to the jury straight without looking at my notes, attempting to recall my deft preparation from the night before. Memory fights back. But I was taking myself by surprise attack; I didn't know until this instant I was going to call her. I wasn't ready, my calculator's triple A batteries were dead. The thoughts were coming so inefficiently. A walk around the room might help. I circled the coffee table and didn't think of anything significant. Then I grabbed my phone like I knew what to do. I didn't waste a second and dialed the complete number, held the phone to my ear. She answered on the third ring. 8 p.m. I was bridging the gap between Radiance and Violet Avenue.

"Hello."

I liked the sound of her voice—peculiar, unidentifiable, but so pretty and worldly.

"Hi, this is Brane."

"Brane . . . who the?" How can anyone mistake a name like mine? But I played along like a dumb shit.

"We met last weekend; don't you remember . . . at Magritte's house?"

"Yes." That's all. This woman didn't sound like the one I met. She was cold, irascible; I was thrown but oddly resolute, deciding not to be offended.

"I thought I'd call since we live near each other, we can walk over to the dinner party tonight. I just assumed you'd been invited, you're a good friend of Franco and Magritte's, aren't you? Maybe we could have a drink along the way?"

"I don't drink."

Everything went right into the context of the first-date compartment.

"You must be dehydrated."

"Did you call me to give me a hard time? I hate sarcasm. How did you get my number?" There was dead silence. "Did Blake give it to you?" Here we go with Blake again.

"I can't recall," I replied, trying to keep myself intact. "Let's go to the Carlisle, there's a decent bar there. I'll pick you up. I'll drink and you can talk."

At that point she became less obdurate, not argumentative, the bar and the hotel rang a bell of security. She then told me a moving story about how she'd lived there as a child and threw a bucket of water on an American president who used to stay there when he visited New York. A little girl from a high floor, dropped a gallon of water on the most important man in the world. Her governess was out of the room. The image came vividly into my mind. It was the second floor and she soaked the president.

She agreed to meet me beforehand and invited me to pick her up. I clicked off and went straight to the typewriter to write:

In 9teen something,
A child checked into,
a hotel on the avenue,
commits an act of aggression,
Later,
The President stepped from his limousine,
Before he entered the hotel.
The little girl from the second floor,
dropped a bag of warm water on the President,
Her arms reached out and let go,
It was not an act of aggression.

Anyway, I knocked it off and dressed in a black suit; one of the few times I thought enough of a date to gear up.

A few years ago I decided I would wear only black; the absence of color appealed to me, but I never bought anything with the intent it'd make me look a certain way. I threw my clothes that weren't black in the trash. Little by little I purchased black substitutes. So, I pulled on a pair of black cowboy boots and a black T-shirt and my black everything. It took me about three minutes to trim my beard, then I stuffed the poem in my pocket and I was off.

CHAPTER VIII

She lived a few blocks from the Carlisle. I walked quickly along Madison, feeling anxious, confident, overconfident. Temporarily I forgot the phone conversation and how she'd made me nervous, unsure of my judgments about any interest she had in me. I crossed Seventy-ninth Street to Park, near where she lived, between Eighty-first and Eighty-second, in one of those apartment houses guarded by a team of doormen who wear caps, white gloves and gold-braided uniforms. They ask you what your name is and who you are calling on, as if you were trying to gain entrance to the CIA in Langley.

The walls of the lobby were white marble, opening into a small sitting room, where I was instructed to take a Queen Anne's wingback chair under a huge gilt-edge mirror supported on both sides by Cupids arching their backs against the frame. That must have hurt. On the opposite side of the room was a fireplace made of carved maple with a keystone in the center. Side chairs of various French and English antique vintages filled the rest of the area. They were all reproductions. It was a goddamn antique boutique. Only a freak like me would notice these details. The room could have used a Bach flute and harpsichord sonata.

The doorman rang her apartment. About five minutes passed, though I hadn't really noticed, until he approached, "There's no answer in Miss Tempest's apartment, would you like to leave a message?"

I raised my head slowly, but not in surprise. I knew she was home. Then the buzzer behind him rang on the board. He swiveled and answered.

"Yes, yes, Madam, I'll send him right up."

She probably did that on purpose, but I was in control of myself and the situation. Nothing was going to throw me. I smiled and got into the elevator with a doorman escort.

We went to the twenty-first floor, one below the penthouse. He waited while I walked down the hallway to her door, the only one on the floor, and rang.

It was ajar. I pushed it, turned back and saw the elevator door closing.

The space inside was bleak, pitch-black. I didn't like that. It made my screwy state of mind feel kind of normal. The apartment door swung back behind me but didn't close. Just a chink of light blinked from the hallway. I didn't say a word, didn't call her name. I was too confused, first the wait downstairs transitioned to darkness.

It lasted a few minutes, until I was just about to say her name. Then I felt something scratch my right hand; was it a sharp comb or brush bristles? I jumped back, not because it startled me, but because it felt inhuman.

My heart pounded, I was scared shitless, reminding me of when I lived in Lesvos. I had a house in Lesvos opposite western Turkey that borders the Mytilini Strait. Minefields were on both sides of the house, separated by a narrow gravel driveway. There was Turkey on a clear day from my front porch. The Turks were to invade any moment to regain Lesvos and other nearby islands. Every time I heard a noise I freaked as the Greek army patrolled the road alongside my house, exploding mines, rocking me around the clock. After going through that, nothing really shook me up until now.

I knew it could only be her, the touch was damn strange.

"You frighten very easily, don't you?" The voice rode through the blackness like I was lost on a back road listening to a late-night radio talk show host.

"Radiance, what's this game? Turn on a light!" I demanded. Then I looked to my left where motorized shades were moving up, the drapes swept to the side. Like a statue she stood by the windows. The city lights illuminated the room. The apartment was on a high floor, it overlooked the park and had a striking view of the reservoir named after Jackie Kennedy in the East Eighties. I was a big JFK fan, growing up in Massachusetts. I walked over to her; I thought she was staring at the West Side. It was uncomfortably quiet and I couldn't think of anything to say, except that's a nice view of the skyline. All I could see was her profile. That hook nose protruded but the rest of her face was covered by her hair. It was combed to hide her other features. Just as I was about to say something, she wheeled around,

"Let's go, we'll be late if we are going to have your drink."

There was no doubt she had been preoccupied. She wasn't really concentrating on me.

"Don't worry about tripping over anything, this room has no furniture."

We were out waiting for the elevator a moment later. I don't remember leaving the apartment or whether she walked in front of me. I was afraid to look at her. Neither of us said a word.

How the hell did I get myself into this and how will it end? One thing was for certain, this wasn't anything like life with Muriel. Now I was in the fast lane.

The elevator arrived. The doorman nervously said, "Good evening, Miss Tempest."

She barely nodded her head and went right behind me. Her shoulders made a birdlike gesture, curling round, angling herself into a corner. When we arrived in the lobby, the other doormen paid their respects; clearly, she intimidated them.

From the time we'd left the apartment we hadn't spoken. I was feeling more and more uneasy—that type of self-consciousness which doesn't come from a first date. I was consciously trying to pinpoint how I felt. For the first time in my life I experienced an eerie sensation. The street didn't look the same. It seemed vertiginous, out of whack. The street lamps dripped fragments of light down to the sidewalk. Everything was moving slowly, I began to feel wind currents, each blowing in a different direction. My eyes glanced at her. She was staring straight ahead, moving forward right by my side. Nothing was disturbing her. All I could see was her profile, the rest of her face was obscured. Her hair was long, trailing down her back. Her coat collar was turned up. She wore a long gray dress, hemmed below her knees.

By the time we arrived outside the Carlisle bar we hadn't said a word. I was feeling vacuous, like I could have floated away. I took a deep, loud breath, attempting to regain my person. Then I felt a biting rawness where something had touched me in her apartment. Parallel vertical scratches were above my wrist. The wounds were open; blood was visible and I was bleeding. At that point I had to decide— either ask her what animal was crawling around her flat or play dumb and find out the hard way. Was it a fucking aggressive cat? As I was figuring it out, I examined my lacerations while her hand nearest me, was moving back and forth. Her nails looked like knives. Again, I felt the wind pushing me, sometimes toward her, then away. What could I do to stop this weirdness? My right hand reached into my suitcoat and I took out the poem and handed it to her.

"Oh, what's this?" she asked with the fake sweetness of a shop girl. "Have you written me a letter because you can't talk?"

"No, that's not a letter." My voice was steady and firm against her sarcasm.

"Tell me, I don't like surprises."

"No, just look at it, read it."

"I won't, I can't stand to be surprised."

"All right," I agreed. "It is something about you and about us."

"Us?" she questioned, shocked. "We don't know each other."

"Read it and we'll discuss that afterward."

This brief conversation allowed me to recover some of my integrity. The wind eased and at the same instant she unfolded the note and began to read it to herself. We were moving toward the hotel entrance. Either she was a slow reader or she went through it several times because she loved literature.

Once inside, a waiter came over and showed us to a table. I ordered gin on the rocks and she went for ice water.

"The poem . . . it's very nice. No one has ever written anything like that for me. But I think it's a little early to be so involved, to be writing a woman poetry." A grin lifted her lips. She watched my reaction carefully.

"You know I'm a lawyer . . . take it in that context. I wasn't attempting to capture anything to do with my emotions. I was only giving you a substitute for something like flowers, just simple words about how you grew up, expressed in a form you might not have seen." I felt good about the way I articulated that line and waited for a positive reaction.

"Are you attracted to me?" she asked, the question came out of her blue.

"No." She was insulted, instantly.

"What do you mean, 'no'? You don't find me attractive?"

"No, I don't think I am attracted to you . . . nor have I thought about whether you are attractive, beautiful that is." Now she was outraged. The face went from inquisitive to ugly.

"Well, what the hell are you doing with me? I hate it when people lie. You're lying, I don't believe a word of what you said. I know you're attracted to me. So, stop playing your childish games. They may work on a dumb model, like the girl from last weekend, but I am nothing like her. I have a brain and I know how to use it! People who just can't be straight, you are despicable!"

The anger was increasing and I was burying my embarrassment, although at the time I was telling her the truth. Something pernicious was toying with my emotions, making me think about her, but I certainly didn't recall ever considering her beautiful or that I was consciously falling for her. So, I defended my position. The waiter brought the drinks, placed them between our third argument. The second one was on the phone and the first at the dinner table, if the discussion concerning the correct means of bringing up children was counted. All the time she was becoming more and more cantankerous, unruly . . . the behavior of a spoiled child. I hate Roquefort cheese and this was a real whiff. I hadn't seen anything like her since I was a kid in grade school listening to one of my bitchy teachers. But, I was probably entertained, forgetting the strange excursion, the scratches on my hand.

Her mood was fucked up and fluid. She asked me, "Do you usually like such strong drinks, gin on the rocks?"

At that moment I had turned my attention to the rest of the bar. I was watching two well-known U.N. diplomats, drinking and talking like old college pals. I didn't listen to her even though I clearly heard what she'd said. Seconds later I motioned for the waiter to bring me the check.

On the way out I said to her, "For the record, I drink gin or vodka when someone is giving me a hard time." She didn't answer, but handed me her coat, expecting me to help her on with it, standing alongside the door.

"Kindly open the door. I insist on being treated like a lady, I assume I am with a gentleman."

The tone was serious and I was going to fucking help her on with her coat and open the door. I didn't laugh as I would have with any other woman. Something in her voice was from another era, try *House of Mirth*. As soon as we were outside I felt those damn winds. This time they were stronger, more insistent on holding me back from moving in any direction. I didn't say anything; she was several feet in front of me on Madison. I stepped off the curb and hailed a taxi.

"Radiance, we're going to be late," I yelled, my coat lifting like a parachute. The cab pulled over, and she got in after me.

"Gentlemen always get into a car first," she advised me.

The same thing occurred as in the elevator. She moved directly against the door, into a corner, shrinking into the angle between the seat and door, like a bird settling into a nest. Yes, of course, I knew all of these events were morbid, but I was witnessing some kind of phenomenon that was so singular I had no frame of reference.

Moments later we arrived at Trick's, an Italian restaurant that I frequented and where Magritte was having her party. Everyone was already seated. From the back of the dining room Magritte noticed us immediately. I felt much better being in the company of a few people I knew but I was surrounded by enemies who didn't know a fucking thing about me. Weren't they all against me? Things settled and became quickly normal as I routinely went from one table to another, shaking hands and making small talk with Magritte, Franco and a number of mutual acquaintances.

Behind me, Radiance was caught up in conversation with the same Italians from the weekend, laughing and gesturing about something Latin. It was strange since she'd mentioned how much she despised Italians and how the sound of their language was crude, lowbrow. I watched her face morph into so many strange expressions just like that. Now it was beautiful, enchanting; seconds before it was anger, disappointment. Her conversation smile was broad, warm and curiously filled with humility. My palms rubbed my eyes, I wanted to make certain I wasn't imagining these transformations. Every minute was different, a brand-new face, fresh out of the box. She shifted her attention to address someone at the back of the table and then she became someone else—homely, sepulchral, evil, all with a slight movement of her head. I blinked, squeezing my eyes shut, then I looked again.

She come to the table, where Magritte had placed our name cards.

We got askance looks from nearly everyone. Again, I thought, we were surrounded by envy and surprise. We were something to talk about.

"Take my coat," she ordered, turning her back to me. Over her shoulders she wore a matronly ribbed cardigan sweater, clearly out of my zone.

Forty people were at the dinner, seated around five large round tables in the back room of Trick's. On my right there was a blonde who didn't know anyone except her date. She struck up a conversation with me right away. Radiance was busy speaking to some other guests. California girl had just landed in New York and wanted to join a ballet company. I gave her my rapt attention because I wanted Radiance to be jealous and to turn the fuck around. After the dancer rattled on I monologued the practice of law and the conflicts between my own problems and my clients' quandaries. She was beautiful, innocent and very sexy, unlike Radiance. Under any other circumstances I would have tried to seduce her; instead, I felt frightened and nervous that Radiance was going to swivel and say something nasty, reducing me to rubble. It was nerve-racking. I couldn't control myself. Although I tried to be attentive in the conversation, I couldn't. My ass was on the edge of the chair. Sure enough, within seconds, I felt the burn of Radiance's eyes on my neck.

"Where are your manners, so rude? Are we supposed to sit here all night not eating? The waiter is standing there very patiently . . . it's time to order." She was right I hadn't noticed the tall, skinny unshaven waiter wearing a thin strand of diamonds tightly snaked around his neck because I was concentrated on the pretty girl. He stared at me as if I was offending Radiance.

Her voice was frosty. I could see the icicles. For the first time I noticed her teeth; she had many. The incisors were sharp, pointed but so did the waiter's. My hands massaged my temples. I smiled. What an odd reaction. I couldn't control my reflexes.

"Well, what would you like, something to start?" I asked nervously. "Why don't you have the escargot?"

"I never eat anything with onions or garlic," she snapped. "You should remember that." Her eyes bore down on me as if I were a trapped roach that had to remember her food and drink.

"Should I suggest something else? I eat here, I know the menu." The waiter seemed to support every nasty sound that came out of her mouth.

"No one chooses my food; I only eat certain things. I am on a very special diet."

Then she glanced at the waiter and said, "Bring me the steak tartare and I'll have spaghetti with tomato sauce for my main course." He smiled then frowned at me.

I ordered and was about to return to the conversation with California girl when Radiance asked again, tapping me on the shoulder,

"So, you are not attracted to me? Do you find her attractive? . . . She's more your type . . . sweet, innocent, blonde hair, clean-cut surfer girl. . . . You can tie her mind in knots."

"I'm having a harmless conversation. First time in New York, that sort of thing. Thought I'd be helpful."

My tone was apologetic. My self-assurance was listing as if were on a ship that was about to capsize. Radiance had manifested so many protean traits in such a short time that I was at my wits' end attempting to make sense out of what was happening. Underneath the artillery being fired at me, I felt connected to her. I couldn't get up and walk away from this total bitch. She was one hell of a lot more interesting than other women. There was no doubt in my mind that no one else in the world was sitting next to anyone like Radiance except me.

She made a heavy sigh, call it a hiss. When I heard that I knew my realm was expanding. It made me shiver. Certainly, there wasn't a problem I had had with women which couldn't be counteracted, combated. I was a master at this game. But this was not a game, no objectives, no winning or losing; all I was trying to do was grasp what was going on, what had happened to her, why she was this way and why I was under such a strain. All my energy was spent figuring her out, for what? I was the one sick and tired of women.

She leaned toward me, snarling, "You are pathetic. I can't stand you!"

Within a split second I snapped, "Fuck you, you bitch. . . . No one has ever said that to me."

I meant it. I'd never been spoken to that way before by anyone and who had?

That startled her. She jumped back, frightened, as if I were going to punch her and I was shaking my fist in front of her face. Our eyes met, mine filled with hatred and hers with waning fear and increasing curiosity. Was she waiting for my next move? I raised myself from the table and started toward the front door, not knowing whether I was going to leave the restaurant or turn around and insult her in front of everyone. As I reached the bar I felt an instant calm. So, she accused me of being pathetic. Big fucking deal. It was meaningless and my rage was a puerile loss of temper. I ducked into the men's room. One urinal. One of those dinner drunks was taking a forever piss. I stood in front of the mirror and waited for his stream to terminate, judging myself, looking for signs of aging, open pores, redness, pimples. Maybe I was pathetic. I had to be honest, whatever masculine pride I had was now questionable. If Muriel would have said that shit to me I would have been long gone. It was now about control, the grip Radiance had on me, but I didn't know that. I'd return to the table and try to discuss things with her instead of scampering out the door like a field rabbit. I shook my head, pissed and found the route back to my seat.

"Steady boy!" I was administering. The boredom and apathy I'd suffered for so long had clearly passed, leaving the brand new me exposed to the blazing sun. How much could I handle? Could I convince myself I was enjoying all the facets of outsmarting her? I would use my head, every art I knew and the refrain of the Fifth repeats in the *Pastoral's* storm so I could quickly learn that there is an ebb and flow and I would be victorious.

What did the rest of the idiots I was sitting with know about risk? This was just another round table for them, where they would drum up the UES dry colloquy of jobs, fashion, vacation and nightclubs. A dress-designing prince was on my left talking on and on about a wooden sailboat he'd recently bought and was planning to sail from Nice to Spain. He was the California girl's walker. Another guy was an international banker who was brooding about exchange rates, how he missed the years he spent in Brussels, unfiltered cigarettes and the perfect white wine. Radiance stared at them disdainfully. Her dark eyes were glowering with an antipathy meant for all of us. I slid back into my seat powerless. The meal had been served.

"I thought you left."

"No, I went to the men's room. Can we work out a rapprochement?"

I started to reach for a cigarette as if I was going to go outside and smoke but I wasn't going anywhere. Then I smiled although I was uncertain in choosing the best expression for her response.

"You're suddenly so French. I can't stand you. You and me, we're totally wrong. It was a mistake for us to meet tonight or any other night for that matter."

The voice was hard but so ironic; it echoed what I said to Muriel hours ago. Maybe she and Muriel were scheming.

"Don't be so impetuous. I'm going to give us some time. There's more to it than you understand."

I started to eat. Luckily, she didn't have time to respond. A surprise guest had arrived whom Franco and Magritte hadn't seen in years. There was an uproar. Seemingly he was a friend of everyone in the room, including Radiance. The party's attention shifted to him.

He was nondescript but that didn't help my anxiety. Franco nudged me and said he was a famous singer from Italy who had been released from jail. The cops in Rome had found kilos of cocaine in his apartment, but it'd been planted. It was a big story in Europe. I returned to my meal and the rest of the Euro trash, watching Radiance out of the corner of my eye. She was eating with her left hand, the right one tucked away. Mainly she picked at the food like a child, carefully choosing the tiny pieces. She didn't like food.

I relished watching her mood grow worse. Each bite brought a grimace. Finally, I couldn't resist.

"What's wrong with the food? Should you order something else?" The humor was obvious, but she didn't react.

"No, this is just fine. I like it," she said.

Her brow and cheeks were perspiring. This wasn't your average person not enjoying a meal; something else was going on. She couldn't eat and was going through the motions to show everyone she could eat prepared food. The eating manner was so weird. She dealt with the plate as if it were a foreign object. Her left arm was crooked, moving up and down like a hoist and she couldn't bend her elbow. Radiance's red lips were puckered, opening a small round space through which slivers of pasta were sucked inside. Her jaws were masticating. I thought of her as an English bulldog at that table. The spaghetti was nearly untouched. She drank a bit of water, again in the same fashion, drawing it in through the hole she'd formed between her lips. My concentration was total, so unnecessarily intense. I'd been hypnotized.

There was a hand on my back. It surprised me and I jumped backward, frightened. Everyone looked at me askance. It was the owner, Angelo, His accent was thick as gorgonzola, born and bred in Chiavari.

"Brane, hour ah you? Gum wit me, der's a gall for you."

He nodded to the table, excused myself, as if anyone cared. We went to the back office, where there was no one, which meant that he wanted to speak to me about something he thought was pressing, which usually turned out to be a bête noire of his. Every time I was there with a woman, he would do this—come to the table and say there was a phone call. Rarely, it was a legal problem about the restaurant and it was an opportunity for free advice. He closed the door and I sat on his beaten-up sofa that he slept on when things were slow.

Not a second was wasted.

"Brane, you're a good boy. . . . I hallways likea you; we know each odda for lotta years? Righta? Righta! Now lemme aska you a somating, OK?"

I didn't have a clue; now I knew it wasn't a legal thing this time.

"Wha da fuck r you doing with dat gunt . . . shesa grazey and dangerous . . . you wanna geda good and fucked up?"

His hands were on his knees, and he was leaning forward. He was so serious it was hard to take him seriously.

"I don't know what you mean." If I told him what had gone on this evening he would have whacked me across the face for lying.

"Wha I know I gannot tell you but dis much I gan."

His voice stopped and he became more somber.

"Every man I ever see her around gets screwed up . . . dey go grazey . . . some of dem even die. Yeah, get grazey in the trangest way or I never see dem again."

I was about to tell him what had happened, but something held me back. There wasn't any reason to, and I felt like I knew better. I'd better get back to Radiance; otherwise, she'd leave. Nothing dawned on me because I had taken my daily stupid pill. What he was saying didn't impress me but it matched up. Who heeds the truth when it's an admonition?

"Angelo, what the hell are you talking about? I have never heard anything so ludicrous. If that were true, I would have known about it by now."

His hands tightened the apron strings around his waist. "You tink so . . . I see a lot more dan anyone . . . I'm here all da time and I been in Noo Yorka a long time. Years ago she lived with a boy name Nicko, dey go to Soud America for two muntz and dey say he fell offa cliff in Peru . . . by accidenta.

Ya, sure. Many people dey tell me da mudda and grandmudda were very differant, 'trange . . . they live togedda in Europe. I tink near da Black Forest in Bavaria. Anyway, so Nicko die, den a little dime later I see her wit a guy I know for years, he's a gooda guy like you . . . I rememba he was in real estate beezieness, had two or tree biga hoffice buildings. And he waza young, no more den terty-five. The next ting I hear about him, he has a disease. It wazzant anyting like gancer, but he wey only bout hundred pounds in da end. Whadever I know I tell you, buta I know she don't loka righta to me . . . someting very evil bout da habits she have. If I waza you I would forget bout her, donut see her no more . . . dere are plenty of good-lookin broads, whada you need her for?"

Now his face was practically against mine. I had never been this serious with him. But it made me laugh, I just couldn't help it. I was just too skeptical and, besides, the mystique I wanted to keep private; I had to have my separate world which I could explore and investigate. There wasn't anything I needed in terms of help right then and there, I stubbornly thought. So, there was no need to pursue the dialogue with Angelo.

"I understand . . . there is nothing to worry about. What can happen? Since you've known me have you ever seen me in a jam I didn't get out of?"

Being cavalier didn't make any impression on him.

He waved his finger at me, like a parent,

"OK, you don't forget whad I tella you dis night. Brane, you are a gooda boy, I like you and dats why I tella you, but you no wanna listen. So whad can I do . . . force you, take you by da ear and putta you in a taxi, zend you home before itsa too late? Believa me, I woulda love justa dat!"

"I'll never be the same . . . I will remember everything you said." By then I was anxious to get back; I was positive she'd be infuriated or possibly she'd left. My mind was bouncing from one circuit to another, all of them red hot, arcing with intrigue.

After I left Angelo in the back room, I saw her from across the restaurant. The Italian actor was sitting in my chair, having a vehement argument with Radiance. I went over and he immediately arose, shook my hand, and said good night to her, kissing her on both cheeks even though there was clearly friction between them.

"Upsetting! The Italians, they are so ignorant I can't believe it . . . that man, he's got the nerve to say that the Communists would be the best thing for Europe. . . . He doesn't know that the first thing they do is stop making movies. Let's leave, I want to go home . . . now. You will get me a cab, won't you?" She didn't have a good grasp of international affairs, and I didn't answer her.

Many of the guests had left; it must have been around twelve-thirty. I wanted to stay. If I could spend some time with her, I thought there'd be more of an opportunity to break down the artificial wall between us. The best thing to do was agree, though I didn't see a method of persuading her, and her ire had been jacked up by the Italian.

"I'll take you home, that's no trouble at all."

She disagreed.

"No, just walk out to the street with me and hail a cab. I want to go straight home . . . alone, the way I should have come. Don't you see? I have nothing, that is, absolutely nothing to say to you. Will you please stop, as of this moment, in persisting? The way you see it and the way I do is just too far apart!"

In reply to that I was quiet. We said goodnight to a few people and walked to the street.

CHAPTER IX

"Let's walk a few blocks; it's cool tonight for a change. I'll get you a cab around Eighty-seventh Street."

She was quiet, seemingly lost in thought, her head bowed. But she followed me a step or two behind, on the pretext of window shopping. After a few blocks she dropped farther back. I kept turning to see if she was still there; then she dashed out to the street and flagged a taxi. Something desperate went through me in that instant; I couldn't let her go like that. The cab approached. Just as she opened the door, I pushed my way between her and the seat.

"What the hell are you doing? I don't want you to go . . . I want to talk to you."

It sounded like I was pleading with her.

"Get out of my way. I already said I want to go home, without you. Look at you, you fool, your fly is open."

Damn, she was right. I yanked up the zipper and nearly let her get away. Surprising myself, I ran over, pushed her away from the moving taxi and I yelled to the driver, "Split! We'll get another cab!"

The bastard didn't move. "Split, man! I said we'll get another one!"

"No, don't leave, don't leave . . . he's crazy!" She called out.

He stopped there, waiting obediently. My hands were gripping her arms like a father controlling an irate child, bending her back over the hood of a parked car.

"I'm not letting you go!" I insisted. At the same time, she yelled back at the cab,

"Don't leave, don't leave!" struggling to break from my hold. What I really wanted to do was turn her loose and beat the shit out of the officious bastard. Thinking about that weakened my concentration. She broke away, laughing, and scooted into the cab. Before she could shut the door, I was in the back seat with her.

"I'm not likely to allow you to say the things you did without getting the chance to tell you . . ."

She interrupted me as her laughter became hysterical and loud. The cab just sat there like a pile of rocks, the driver waiting for an address.

The laughter subsided into a wicked silence,

"Brane, you are mad. You should forget this, it won't do you any good to take me home." Then her sinister laugh prevailed.

I imitated Muriel, "I want to talk to you. I know there's something great between us, we can talk about it. . . . Don't tamper with it now. This is much too early."

What the hell was I blabbing about? I couldn't understand myself. There wasn't any real difference from my thoughts last weekend—she was damn homely to me. I couldn't be attracted to her. Again, she glued herself into the corner of the cab like a frightened reptile and whispered, "Eighty-fifth and Park."

I sat back and thought I wasn't going to give up, I was that determined. As we drove down the avenue, my face must have been as serious as Napoleon at Waterloo, while she kept taunting me with her nonstop sarcastic laughter, bringing on a sick hiccup. When I think back about what happened, I now know her rejecting me was the direct result of me seeing her as ugly and pathetic. She knew exactly what I was thinking. The pallor of her skin, the desperation, the loneliness, the homely face and the sadism. Where did this creature come from?

Then we were in front of her building. I tried to suppress the hiccups. A doorman ran out and opened and stood by while I gave the prick driver the fare in small change without a tip. Before I could climb out of the back seat, she was in the lobby. I ran inside, catching her at the elevator.

"C'mon with me, I want to say a few things to you." Then I hiccupped. Shock, she agreed,

"All right, just stop doing that offensive thing with your throat!"

She turned and went out to the sidewalk. No one was there except us and the doorman, who stared our way.

"All right, what is it?" She leaned against the building and folded her arms. Once again, the acid frown, those psychotic eyes, and the waxy pale skin tone. The hiccups were gone.

"Nothing, just nothing, it was all a mistake. I can't put my finger on exactly what this is, but if you give us a day or two, we can have something incredible together. Trust me."

This was another bad imitation of Muriel. Trust me, what the hell was that? Surprisingly, she made no effort to return to the building and she was listening. I suggested we go back to the bar and just talk and she agreed. From that point, her disposition changed, she was becoming sweet, call it cute.

When we were seated, she said, "I haven't met anyone so persistent. You must be interested, and I'm complimented.

"That's a far cry from telling me earlier you weren't attracted to me!"

"The truth is I am not attracted to you."

That reply should have sent her right back to her apartment. But it didn't. What was happening was an exploration of myself, an attempt to understand my feelings.

It was 2:30 a.m. and we'd discussed our old relationships, sensitivity, honesty and all the other table settings that make man and woman compatible. The bartender was cleaning up, getting ready for closing, counting the night's receipts. Her chin was resting on her hands. Our old arguments were obscured and I was content to overlook what occurred. I'd recovered some of my shattered ego. Before she could say let's leave, I initiated it.

"Better be on our way, you look worn out . . . you're practically falling asleep. Anyway, this place is closing." I helped her on with her coat.

Outside she turned to me,

"I had a lovely time. I feel you were right in many of the things you said. I'm glad you got into the cab with me, didn't let me go."

"So am I." She kissed me, her lips pushed against mine while her hands remained tucked into her coat's pockets. It felt soft, affectionate, but curiously ice cold. She stepped back, almost smiled, then she laughed as if one could read the word laugh, and then I walked her home.

The time was 3:30 a.m.

I went home feeling a strange sense of accomplishment. Using all of my emotions and my skilled sculpting of language, I had turned the evening around and regained to some extent the old reality, assured of my status with women. It didn't last long. When I was in my bedroom, I undressed, climbed into bed. I wasn't tired so I grabbed a book and read a bit, until her name began to occur at the start of each page.

"Should I call her?" I asked myself and pondered whether or not it was best to leave well enough alone. Moments later I phoned, not having the slightest idea as to what I would say. She answered as if she knew I would call.

"Hello," there was that sweet voice again. It wasn't sleepy.

"Radiance, it's me."

It wasn't what I wanted to say.

"Only called to tell you I had a great time, I think you're terrific." Shit, that was lyrical.

"What are you doing?"

"Getting ready to go to bed," I replied, matter of factly, how fucking dull.

"Alone?"

"Yes, what do you think, I met someone after I left you?"

"No, do you want to come over here. Do you want to make love to me?"

The past me, the ass man, was of no consequence, no help, when Radiance said it, that was a go. The evening's final extrapolation coming at four o'clock in the morning after all the tests had been run. Well, I wasn't even certain I wanted to make love to her, hadn't given her one sexual thought. Nevertheless, I couldn't tell her that!

Before I knew it, I said, "Yes," and she replied, "Then get your ass over here!"

There I was back on the avenue, this time thinking about my prospective hard-on. She was ugly. Radiance Tempest was certainly not going to settle for something on the soft. I still wasn't attracted to her but I was getting hard.

This wasn't going to be embarrassing. The typical excuses men make to women. The bastard had a mind of its own and it was oddly choosey. It was becoming more and more invested with a separate set of responses. I could be watching a radiator and get stiff and be with the greatest-looking woman and have to roll over and go to sleep. I just didn't know what type of dilemma that fucking root of mine was going to put me in next from time to time. All of it was related, I theorized, to the phobia I created of disinterest, culminating with Muriel.

Step by step on the street, figuring out the geography of the moment. First, we'd enter some form of embrace, put our lips together, then my hands, her hands, would run over our body parts. At some point we'd be on the couch, the floor, roll over and I'd be on top of her. I'd make an excuse, "Let's go to the bedroom." But that would buy me only a short amount of time. Like most women, the odds were she would want to go to the bathroom first. More time, I'd play with myself, get an one warmed up. Who knows, at that moment my mind might begin to play its miscellaneous games in conspiracy with my prick. Making me think of other women, of locomotives, rare books, anything to distract from the real business of proving my virility. If I were only a kid just wanting to get laid, blindly, nothing more or less. Just want to score, get in a hole so I could tell the corner boys about it. No, it wasn't like that anymore; the great conquests weren't talked about; it was boringly commonplace. The important matter of feeling wasn't there. That's hard to get up.

I'm in the lobby, and the doorman, the same one who'd seen me on the three other occasions this holy night, is ringing her apartment. The consent comes through the house-phone wires, permission to get fucked, granted by the queen from the palace boudoir. The elevator ascends and the door is unlocked, the elevator descends. I penetrate the same darkened quarters. Again, the room behind the innocent door is opaque. A split-second passes and I see the light at the end of the tunnel—a small corridor leading to a room which is lit with the soft lights of a distant ocean liner.

Radiance is sitting, lighting a cigarette, like a swarthy Turkish smuggler in a cafe in Istanbul. Thick swirls of smoke float toward the ceiling. We examine one another silently. This confrontation is for the prearranged matter of the sure thing. My brain investigates her sexuality for the first time, and she does the same. Damnit, she's homely, and I have not been to bed with that many homely women, but suddenly her looks don't seem to make any difference.

I am there, I have to do something. She moves toward me and I sit next to her on the couch.

"Are you attracted to me? . . . I have my Ethiopian wedding dress on." A smile as wide as her head stares at me. Never have I seen anything as grotesque. All those teeth and the exaggerated face . . . the clown's red lips beckoning me into the fun house.

"Don't be afraid of this thrill, don't be afraid," I hear said in tones growing softer, putting me aboard a ship on a cruise across a white ocean. The waves roll like yards of silk in the wind. I am being enchanted, captured by what I have to tell myself is just one of God's creatures, just like me. The ship is rolling, a ballet in space, I believe I am getting seasick; I feel the lightness rising in my stomach. It stops right there, and I feel high, but I choose to let go and be taken beyond. The limited shape of it. Here's where I could have made my first mistake. I think I let go of myself then; I just wanted to release my suffering self. Where the hell was everyone else? Eating that same stupid salad, drinking wine, worrying about life? Well, I wasn't, I was in one of the places where money buys nothing. The land where people don't have to say anything.

I was falling in love.

Shit, it had been so long. Those fingers were running through my hair as she began to move toward me with those lips like a battering ram and then her tongue was deep inside, to the bottom of my throat. I was choking with lust, and I want to die from it. Simultaneously, something intangible still disgusted me about her. A quality even the most lascivious whores usually don't have is present. Radiance was vulgar! My hand was between her thighs and we were on a journey. Smooth, so smooth it didn't feel like any other human I'd ever touched. What was it? I couldn't take my hands away. She had an enormous organ, I could have easily put my fist inside.

What was I doing with her? This dress she wore was a filthy rag. It was damp, probably old sweat, but I was smelling like a clammy dog. The pain in my back was gone. One thing I knew for certain—this was no ordinary booty call. The conflicts were frightening. I became more obscenely fascinated, intrigued, than afraid. That night I would've boarded a spaceship to nowhere with her.

The tongue lagged in my mouth, pushed downward; I felt like it'd come out of my ass. I didn't know what to do, my body and mind were under siege, overrun by barbarians cutting off everyone's heads in the village. My system was over-engaged and I couldn't resist. We moved toward another room; I thought it must be a bedroom. The hallway was too dark. One of her arms was around my neck and halfway down my back. I felt enclosed in a shell, a shroud, a cowl thrown over my head. Maybe it wasn't her arm, but I didn't care, even though it pushed me forward like a rifle barrel prodding a prisoner. I thought I heard an electronic sound, a barely audible beeping in a pattern, one short sound, one long, followed by one short and another long. Was I in iambic pentameter hell? Where was the beeping coming from? I'm afraid to guess, but I swear it was being created by Radiance.

A few seconds later, I was on my back. I couldn't see her face and the room was quiet. She was thrashing around, I imagine, taking her clothes off.

My hands reached back and felt two pillows and a cold wall. Being in a bed was comforting; at least it appeared all we were going to do was just make love. Just.

I couldn't care less what happened; I was so far into this adventure nothing mattered. I was prepared to spend the rest of my life out of my mind without a grain of sanity. Then the pulse of the beeping started again, coming closer to me, and fading as if someone were playing with the volume. Nothing was visible; I didn't remember ever being anywhere. My clothes were on the floor, but I didn't take them off. There was a macabre, baleful silence, plus a slimy, humid room temperature. Suddenly, the silence was broken; I could make out a silhouette of what looked like Radiance at the foot of the bed. Her voice sliced through the blackness.

"Brane . . . can you hear me?" The sonar pulsing stopped.

"Yes," I replied, shaking from the chill.

"What is your greatest fantasy?"

Here we go again. Fantasy, a threesome with two goats, a parrot and Siamese twins?

"I have no fantasies."

"Come on, tell me . . . you must have just one, what is it?"

"I said I don't have any. Can't we stop this and just have a cheese sandwich?"

There was no response from her this time. The silhouette began to move, gyrate. I could hardly see what was going on. The sound of birds chirping was all around me, echoing as if we were in a cave. I could hear water droplets, splashing like they were falling from the ceiling into pools or was it spilling out of a bucket of blood? A musty odor filled the room, making me instantly hold my nose. I tried to breathe through my hand, but it was no use; it jammed my nostrils—a heavy putrefying perfume. Then it came, the flapping sound the wings of a vulture make. I could feel gusts; I swear I saw two huge wings being raised and lowered hovering over me like a pterodactyl. Franco and Magritte were lying next to me, their teeth in my neck.

"You thought we just threw dinner parties, well that's not all," Magritte whispered.

"This is the specialty of our country house," Franco was quick to add. It was no time for idle conversation.

I pushed them away. My hands reached forward for protection, feeling stiff hairs on this beast's legs because it was hovering. Suddenly it was on top of me spreading itself across my face. I want to scream but that was out of the chilling question. The words wouldn't form. The odor intensified and I could barely breathe. It was intoxicating and I was getting hard goddamnit.

Radiance, this couldn't have been her, she must have left the room. My hands gripped thighs, they were furry and heavy. I felt like a spelunker, cornered by the horror he observed from a distance. Then I knew it was her. I felt that scratching thumb and suddenly there they were, two more raking my ribs—Franco and Magritte. I'll be godamned, I knew they were strange. Suspended in the air directly above me was Radiance, gesturing, floating. I didn't want my prick to be inside this thing that was thrashing on top of me. A thing that was beeping, pulsing at a fantastic rate until it faded to ultrasonic.

This was ecstasy. Then it was just her and me, wherever Franco and Magritte went I'll never know but there was blood all over my neck.

Christ, I must have had a mammoth coronary. I was dying with fright and pleasure. I couldn't breathe; it made me vomit. But I had a colossal orgasm, sperm running over my legs, and I felt the hair on the beast's legs wet from a cum typhoon.

CHAPTER X

I put a pillow behind my head and turned over to look out the window. It's morning, and Radiance, looking so uncharacteristically beautiful, is asleep on her side next to me in her bedroom. The sun is out; try that on for size. Things seem so fucking cozy. Did I survive last night or was it a dream?

I didn't want to wake her, so I quietly slipped out of bed. My clothes were neatly folded on an armchair in the corner. Was this where we were last night? I was too intimidated to ask. First thing, I touched myself, just to make absolutely certain this wasn't a dream, maybe a hallucination. Sure enough, I was alive, and I was there.

Fatigue covered my mind. I tried to yawn through it and stretch quietly. She's lying on her side in a white cotton nightgown, breathing gently; the covers are tightly tucked in as if she'd merely slipped into a made bed. I can't reconcile the tranquility with last night. This is the high art of deception. Perhaps I am barking mad. The room is beautiful. The bed frame is bamboo and two enormous, tufted, wine-colored armchairs are on either side, which are bordered with hand-carved mahogany panels illustrating villagers doing chores. A glass lamp stands near the windows over a desk full of tiny compartments and drawers with hand-painted veneers. The girl has taste.

Tiptoeing, I grabbed my clothes and went out to the living room like a fucking elf. As I dressed, I tried to recall the dimensions of this room when I picked her up Thursday night. Now it was full of furniture: two white couches perpendicular to a fireplace; between them, an Indian rug thrown over the parquet floor; along the window there was a Victorian lounge on which were pillows, covered in mink and leopard skin. Top-notch NYC decorators worked this place over. I checked the view of the reservoir. It hadn't changed. From behind I heard someone coming toward me; I spun around expecting the worst.

"Would you like breakfast, sir? Good morning, my name is Otis . . ."

This plot pusher who is towering over me was the houseboy. Obviously, he must have been the guy Blake saw Radiance with on Madison and he was all of six-feet-six, wearing a shark's tooth necklace and a chamois waistcoat opened over a bare, ripped chest. He should have been at a bodybuilding competition. The definition of each leg muscle bulged against his black tights.

His hands were clasped together in a servile gesture, but had he said, "Get your ass in the kitchen and make breakfast," I would have whipped it right up.

"Sir?" he repeated softly, his hands washing one another; call it mild impatience.

"Yes, I would just like coffee, cream and sugar. "

I almost said "nothing," fearing a stitch of arsenic, but I wanted to see everything I could while I was still there. It was like I was begging for something peculiar to happen to reinforce, to prove, last night.

"That'll be ready in a moment; are you sure you don't want anything else? I can cook anything you like, eggs and toast?"

I shook my head and stared at his flashing eyes. They were like strobes, but at the same time I felt he was harmless.

From the living room, I watched Otis lumber into the kitchen

"Is she sleeping or just pretending?" That was now the question I blurted out.

I started toward the bedroom, trying to catch a glimpse of her again. Just as I pushed the door, Otis stepped in front of me, placing a large hand across the jamb like it was a two-by-four.

"Sir, you're not to disturb Miss Radiance. . . . She is resting. Your coffee is ready."

There was a frightening choice: Treat him like a servant—tell him to get lost—or obey. I pushed the door open all the way and tried to move forward. The room was pitch-black.

The sunlight that filtered through the curtains was gone. Are they trying to drive me mad? His arm was around my waist, guiding me back to the living room. Now in a docile tone of voice, staring into my eyes, he muttered, "The coffee is getting cold."

His arms were folded across his chest and he stood in the bedroom hallway. I went to the lounge, sat down, pursed my lips and poured a cup. There was fruit in a silver gadrooned bowl, not the type one usually eats in New York. Apricots, mangos, a nectary selection. Bat food. While I sipped the coffee, I couldn't help looking up at him after each gulp. He seemed to be concentrating on an internal exercise; his breathing was an asthmatic octave lower than snoring. The eyes were glaring at no particular object, maybe the wall opposite. Had I dropped in on a mad scientist's guinea pig?

What else was there to do? How could I tell when she'd awake? I wasn't going to stay here all day with this madman. If I wanted to kill a few more minutes, I could have eaten some of the fruit. Although each piece was ripe, beautiful, none of it appealed to me because it was sinister. It had been picked from the garden of evil. One thing was sure, I was now leaving. Otis followed me to the door.

From behind I heard him say, "Have a nice day," as I walked out to the hallway. His definition of "nice" deserved to be mounted on a plinth. My confused brain asked, how could I leave at a time like this?

Before Otis closed the door, I slipped back inside.

"Yes, sir, did you forget something?" He stood in front of me with his hands folded in back of him.

"No, but I want to wait for Radiance to wake up," my hands gesturing explanatorily.

"Is that what you want?" He smiled. "That's easy. Why don't you sit on the couch and have more coffee?" Just like that.

I started to walk but my feet felt heavy, immovable. The bastard put something in the coffee. My arms were lead suitcases; I tried to turn to him, but the neck bones were not cooperating.

Shit, I was late for work. . . I'd forgotten today was Friday and I had meetings all day. What time was it? I'd ask Otis. There wasn't anyone in the room. Otis? He was no longer. Thousands of snowy mountains were around me, green valleys and pink water. Harlequins standing on each summit cracking their whips. I'm standing on a deflating balloon, I will be in the water. My arms are covered in bite marks, craters from carnivorous insects.

Pregnant women approached, each claiming I was the one and the only way to stop them was taking responsibility for each of these unborn children. They were calling me "father." It was a joke, wasn't it? So, I laughed. Their black-and-blue stomachs protruded from rouge maternity gowns monogramed with my initials. Oh my God, what have I done with my life, not this! The bastards have drugged me, what for? The marks are itching, gutting me, I can't stop ripping skin, a keyboard of bleeding divots, as if I'd been sprayed with buckshot.

Radiance! I have to find her; she must be here! The water is too deep; I'll drown and there are so many mountains to climb, climb every one. But I can't stay here; I'll be eaten alive. Where are those sadistic insects, just one? It's invisible, flying parabolically between my legs and arms. What does he want? I'd readily give him a quart of my blood. The sky is still blue; thankfully, color will keep me within the boundaries. There is light, so much 24-carat gold light from this afternoon, but no sun in the clear sky. No, I don't prefer to backtrack to the quotidian regularity, the rhythm of Muriel. Reason has lost the struggle against the irrational. The water is not deep, I will not drown; it's waist level; the sand is soft under my feet. In the distance, I see her bedroom and I know I can swim that far. My hand is on the doorknob, twisting it back and forth. Locked. As fate would have it, a storm is brewing. These ocean winds are tossing me around, the waves thick. I can't swim through syrup.

"Don't panic," I tell myself, but the fear is coiled, knotted in my breast. Will I simply die of fear, not the experience? This is terrible, my shirt is wet, and I am bound to catch a cold and I don't have any chicken soup. I can't afford to get sick at a time like this, I have to watch what is going on. If I miss a minute, I won't be able to put it together. Understanding, yes, there will be an explanation for every tiny detail. I have to get out of the place and feel the air. I can't sit here forever; I'll drive myself mad. My elbows are touching the walls; why did I hire such a small room? More area, Lebensraum, that's what I need and another drink.

Not that coffee, Otis, I know what's in it. One thing is for certain, I don't make the same mistake twice . . . not immediately. While I am at it, I'd like to know just who procured, who employed, me to do this? Reveal yourself to me! If I run my hands through my hair once more, I'll pull out every follicle. Remind me to stop biting my nails just when they begin to look good. There are so many things to think about;

The Dream's dreamer
sees what is going to
happen.
Countersunk
up to my head,
sticking outside the glacier
wall, disintegrating.
Riding the flames and ashes
of Destiny's volcano.
Forced to the earth's axis
on the center of the lion's
breath of fury.
Screwed into the center of
the planet, one with one.
Swallowing the ocean whole
and entering the Dragon's
head.
There is no thought that
will survive, inexperienced.
No fear will avoid its
Master. No bee will be hived,
No rhyme will stay unconnected
to its reason.
Life is just the neophyte's
beginning. The indoctrination.
Pain and torment are the infants
of an ancestry of beasts who
know nothing but the administration
of what reaches beyond

capacity.

Death is the doorway—not to heaven,
not to hell—to another
life unconscious, felt for an
unforgettable second that grips
the soul bypassing the body.

There has to be some safety, a raft, a dock, a wharf. No one dies like this, swimming round a living room of sea water, anywhere on Fifth, Park Avenue or the upper east side. Better swim back and try Radiance's door. I'll break it down if I have to. This time the knob turns easily and I walk in, but it's not her bedroom. There's a reception desk and a clerk with sparkling eyes, blond hair and a toothbrush mustache waiting with a ready pen for me to sign the register. He doesn't want any of my identifying documents, only the first night in advance.

"This is The Rand Hoteldorf. You will be in Room Thirteen . . . a small, pleasant surrounding with a balcony overlooking the hotel and two flowerpots next door."

"Can I see the room first, try before I buy?" I say again.

"Certainly."

Then he showed me every room, even ones with guests waking, brushing teeth, arguing with themselves, others eating round biscuits from square packages and guests returning from the hallway.

"Thirteen will be fine," I say again, even though there's no sink, shower or closet in the room. There is one light switch. I decide I can get used to anything by now. "I think I'll enjoy my stay here at The Rand Hoteldorf," I tell Hans.

He is not nervous. The pressure he feels from checking in unpredictable guests disappeared long ago, but he doesn't know what I am capable of during my indeterminate stay. This time it is serious. I will be here for some period during which I will see a doctor every day and take therapy to new heights. After so many attempts, I have decided I don't want to die anymore. Life is necessary even if it is not precious. The slide from moment to moment is beginning to fascinate, nourish me.

What I don't want is to figure out or measure each of her thoughts and ways of appearing to me when in reality she does not have me on her mind and is not going to be with me. Don't torture me by her absence! Make a new man out of me and send me into the field with the infantry; I am getting wounded because I am too close to the enemy. Contact with her is intricate, twisted and sick. The hotel is my retreat, refuge and center of meditation, where I cannot be located except over loudspeakers by my physician. But I can remain secret, balled up into the gaseous unknown, a streak of white mist, slipping up and down these corridors. I can easily become nothing more than the space between two nurses and their quartz watches, because they know I am the indispensable part of my breakdown.

At last, he left me to my room. That was not something he is obliged to do, he could have stayed. After all, he is the receptionist. His duties never end. We are all on our own here and we pay for it. No one renders this guided service free of charge. I am lucky because in large cities they leave your dead body in the basement, behind the boiler, if anything goes wrong with their hotel.

All this goddamn running around the room is killing my back. I can hardly move my arms, and each bone of my fucking vertebrae feels as if it were stuck to flypaper fluttering in a hurricane. Literally, my body is falling from grace along with its former perfect health. Like everyone, I, too, am hitched to aging; the well-known abhorrent process! You'd think whoever is in power would have a more advanced imagination. Life should be transferred to death. Withering into liquid soft tissue, day after day, room after room, piano note onto happy hour cocktails. Then the music stops. How long will my frame occupy my stall at The Hotel Randolphe? Radiance, you livid bitch, mistress of the soporific, wake and tell me that last night and now in this flophouse is just a dream of mine. . . . Let's go back to the moment I was leaving Muriel behind and contemplating nothing, nothing, nothing like this.

This woman! Radiance, are you the bitch, the one who makes all the demands in Room Twenty-two? There is no way I can reverse "Twenty-two" and come up with anything different. I see what you will become. Age, that's what you need, Radiance. You must be suppressed, confined to this hotel as I am, eating specks of crumbled chocolate, washing it down with tepid Diet Coca-Cola. No excursions to the world outside for you, no ticket to travel anywhere. You, like me, have had your sanity passport canceled. The days are over when you could attract me because you could sting like a hornet, your thespian beauty escaping identity. I am the actor, this is my tragedy, you are not included.

This woman Radiance. Yes, Radiance is the bitch; the one who makes the demands that emanate from Room Twenty-two. The palindrome of twenty-two, of Radiance and me and of Radiance and the old hag in Room Twenty-two. If I could unravel that hag, I could find Radiance somewhere underneath the mortiferous, ancient cobwebs of womanhood. I could find myself.

Now the bastard pain is in my foot, a dull aching that requires a bottle of red delivered to my room. I will pay with my last few crumpled dollars. These complaints are all bullshit; one room is just like any other. A theory which doesn't seem to hold very much water in the flat of Ms. Radiance Tempest, a veritable merry-go-round conductor of the bizarre. Maybe she's just hanging around this abode with Otis, doing the Australian crawl through my medulla oblongata. Where am I? But there is one elongated feeling with which I am familiar . . . this queer fucking pain now stretching from the top of my right shoulder, along a turnpike, to the bottom of my two feet. The manual says half of it is sciatica. I continue and think I haven't rubbed pain the wrong way by complaining.

They must have sent up the chambermaid, rather the chamberboy. No women work here. It is not permitted! Just gay men exerting themselves toward me, using every form of body suasion to cajole me. Should I persist in opening Radiance's door and crossing the threshold of horror or reside in Room Thirty-one, waiting to find my sexuality sedated by another sexuality? The spine of intrigue challenges me in diffusing the infinite feminine ignition, which turns the quenchless engine of dissatisfaction. I am fascinated; I will stay, and I am not really entertained, but death is not my first choice. The test of my purpose is written, a mandate. The drug is wearing off.

A few moments ago, I tried to check out of The Hotel Randolphe. Hans said it was all right to do so, but that I would never be permitted to get out of The Rand Hoteldorf. What's the circular use? I remain. Anyway, how could I afford to leave? The management knows so much about me.

Ah, but yes, I possess only myself, since the devil applies his technique only to those who are for sale. I will not sell out to Otis and let him, or his mountains and ocean, block me from finding out what she is doing in that bed. The supernatural is not applicable, not joined to her astral cord, like the normal us. She, too, will arise and eat a mundane breakfast of toast, eggs, and coffee. Won't she see the day, foot to forehead, her energy crumbled into fatigue, light blemished by darkness? Will not her transitory head lift off the pillow, emerge around the corner of the green blanket and desire the comfort of a new day's sun? She breathes, walks. . . I saw that, I spoke and ate with her. We asked and answered one another's questions. The world is real as defined by my compulsory and voluntarily educated curiosity. No longer can I wait impatiently in the thick of this neurosis.

I am going into her world out of the hotel.

Why is it taking so long to descend the steps of The Hotel Randolphe? All I have to do is reach no more than twelve inches and push the door open, but the air is granite to my aggressive touch. I want it too much; I want this next event. Grab the future, swallow it like oasis water down my leathery parched throat. Again, my dear boy, there is no choice, I am to wait. The air must be cleared and then I can try the door. The standstill compels me to contemplate the pain, that of the body, the mind, the wait. How do I entertain the insistent demands of the cathode mind repelling repetition, embarking like a sparrow recovering from the grasp of a human hand? Set me free.

Otis. The giant is in front of me again. "More coffee, sir?" Who the fuck is he, Mr. French Roast? Those eyes are not giving me a choice and his white fingertips are caressing the ends of the shark's teeth in his necklace.

Isn't he satisfied that I am doped up enough? I am going to fight, refuse to eat or drink anything else.

"No. Is there a phone in the kitchen?" I ask in my naive voice, hoping he will drift with the change of the subject. "It must be noon; I have to phone my office."

It was the truth. I am a responsible attorney, and my secretary should know the whereabouts of her employer. Maybe there is an emergency. A judge may have phoned. One of the many possibilities requiring my presence in the law office could have occurred. So, what! I wasn't leaving for work.

The only reason I broke my neck as a lawyer was to meet women like Radiance, wasn't it? Isn't a man's work a quest for recognition? To be with a woman who is sought after by competitors . . . men of stature and ambition.

Now I was clear again. The drug had worn off. Then I remembered something else about Radiance from a New York gossip column.

"Some of the richest men in the world would give Radiance Tempest anything—a private jet, villa in the south of France, diamonds galore just to be seen with her." A worldwide demand for her. Possibly true.

But I was local, goddamn conscious of Otis and the obstruction his filthy figure created between me and the door.

My cell was dead.

"Can I use the house phone," I humbly asked.

"Certainly, feel free to use the phone. Do you need some paper, a pen?"

Those lips moved like lava, the softness underscoring his schooled constraint.

He did frighten me, but I followed his direction. Perhaps his effect was designed only for the suppression of disagreement. FBI agents use the same technique. "I appreciate that, Otis," I said, pressing my lips together and tilting away from him in an attempt to get him to follow me for a change in the direction of the kitchen. It didn't work; he stepped to the right and put out the flat of his hand without touching me.

"If you please, sir, I am only allowed in the kitchen; there is a telephone in the guest room . . . just to the rear of where you are now standing."

Turning my head, I saw the door to the room where Radiance and I first romanced. It was half opened. The room was just as we had left it, except I am sitting on a couch outside without her.

"Will that be all, sir?" he peered into my eyes from the threshold. "And what about some more coffee? It is no problem for me, I have a pot brewing."

Now he was posing like a mummy, arms folded rigidly, indicating I was not to leave, I was governed by houseboy law. Otis walked to the phone, picked up the receiver and asked, "Sir, what is the number of your office? I'm happy to dial it for you."

"I can do that."

"I insist. Miss Radiance keeps a record of each call."

Ignoring him, I began to dial the number. He pressed the receiver against my fingers.

"As I said, I will be glad to call for you. . . . What's the number?" His waxen smile, his chalk-white front teeth were disgusting but resolute.

The choice was clear. I took a shot at his gut. Like a spectator, he watched my fist move and didn't make an effort to avoid the impact. His muscles didn't flex fast enough to protect him and, just as I hoped, he doubled over, coughing to catch his breath while offering the top of his head to be smashed with anything I could get my hands on. I picked up a heavy crystal ashtray, full of last night's butts, whacking him squarely on his skull. The glass exploded with contact. No one could have survived that. His body swiveled, he groaned and sat next to me on the couch, like a drunken sailor on shore leave. Otis was out cold. No way I could take that back; I'd have to bear her wrath. Well, he wasn't dead, although the blow probably would've killed anyone else.

Then I phoned; my secretary answered.

"Brane, where are you? I've got a hundred things to speak with you about. . . . You know it's nearly two o'clock."

Before I could say anything, she put the receiver down and gathered the mail and messages. It gave me a moment to remember how screwed up I was dealing with law office order. The two—me and the office—were as compatible as oil and sand. Once I heard her reciting my name, I wanted to hang up. My brain was in no condition to deal with the easiest case. But I'd get everything ironed out with Radiance.

"Let me see," she began, "you were supposed to be at a meeting in Michael Dwyer's office about the Phillips deal at 11:30; Ms. Morris waited for you at 9 a.m. for about twenty minutes, but she had a dentist's appointment, so she left angry. You are scheduled for three things this afternoon in your diary, at two-thirty, three-forty-five, and a late meeting with some film producer at six for drinks in his suite at the Sherry Netherland. Shall I run down the list of your calls? Three of your paying clients insist they speak with you immediately."

She knew how to emphasize the word *paying*. For a moment I held my cellular in my hand, staring at Otis, a breathing mass of animal, thinking what all of my clientele would do if they could witness this scene. I didn't want to know what was waiting for me if I called anyone back; I couldn't get myself pulled together and all of it seemed too remote. My practice was a frog croaking in a pond, miles away, vaguely disturbing my afternoon nap.

"Forget it, call them all back and tell each of them that I am tied up in a difficult trial in federal court which may last until the end of the month or God knows when."

"What about these meetings, shall I cancel them?" she asked hurriedly, knowing that I was in no mood to work.

"Can them!" I said as if I were never coming back.

"Should I make new appointments for next week?" This time she sounded worried about me instead of the stability of the office. I didn't answer for a moment, appreciating her, which was something I should have started doing years ago.

I laughed, "No, for the time being just let things go. . . . When I return, I'll work it out." After agreeing with me, she hung up while I sat back on the couch inhaling deeply.

A large bump, in the shape of a soup spoon, was on Otis' head, which had pushed its way cleanly through his short hair. More than a headache was in store for him. Whenever he came out of the galaxy under that lump, I was certain there was to be something extra-special devised for me. Now that I was in the center of this adventure, I had to act the part. Tie his legs and his wrists, and gag him. He looked so damn dumb with the shark's teeth crisscrossing one another on the folds of his neck, his huge chest heaving. With every bit of my strength, I rolled him onto the rug, lowering him like a duffle bag. Dead weight. I ripped the wire out of the wall and hogtied him, hand-tied him and loved every minute of seeing him so weak and helpless. There was hardly enough cord to complete the knots. The last thing I did was ball up the cloth napkin from the coffee tray and stuff it in his mouth. I should have poured one of his infamous cups down his throat, but I couldn't think of everything. I was anxious to get to Radiance.

All I had to do was reach for the bedroom doorknob, turn it, and I would be with her, wake her, and find out once and for all what the hell was going on. I froze, like a performer sick from stage fright. The scuffle with Otis hadn't strengthened my purpose; its aftereffects put the thump in my heart. I stood in the hallway, watching her door, trying to sort out, break down the fear. Once again, I examined her image. It smiled at me like the old lady in Twenty-two. Over and over again I replayed the memory of her at Trick's. Her look of disgust.

Suddenly it all became meaningless, unimportant, like a cramp that has come and gone. No reason to wonder endlessly; I wasn't going to do anything about it like call a psychiatrist, tell him I was holed up like a criminal in a large flat on Park Avenue with a sleeping beauty and an unconscious houseboy. Could you make a house call and shrink me? By the way, could you check out my unconscious friend here, tied up like a rodeo steer, the one with the swollen head? No, I just have to go on, ascend the next plateau, but it was not to be simply that, merely opening a door and having a conversation with the inhabitant. Was there an explanation for Otis? What temp employment agency was he registered with? Did Otis really do anything out of the ordinary except spike the coffee or was that a result of my contact with her or more frighteningly . . . my lack of sanity that equals insanity? I was losing the ability to distinguish facts, to put them in an order; my head felt like a racetrack: horses, cars, motorcycles, speedboats running around on water, dirt, concrete, turf.

And what was I going to say to her for openers? Did you sleep well? That is, if she were awake and, if not, should I wake her? It occurred to me that the reason I hadn't feared Otis was because I was overwhelmed with my fear of her, my fear of losing her. I didn't know what I'd made love to last night or what made love to me. Or if it ever happened. The only proof I possessed was Otis telling me she was still sleeping, didn't want to be disturbed. I knew I slept in that room.

1. I am a conscious being, one who makes a minute-by-minute assessment of what is happening and how I am digesting all of it, like a credit card that is infinitely charged for goods and services. How long could I stand in the hallway trying to reach a conclusion about when I would open that door? As I attempt to recall everything in its filthy entirety, I cannot recall that I am seriously human and very frequently seduced by daydreams. Buddy, this was no musing. Instead of laboring over all the items which my brain pondered, I will consider only the essence. . . .

2. I was a bather in front of the wave, uncertain about water temperature, unsure of his skill as a swimmer; he feels the waves crash at his feet, where

he is safe. He inches in, wades up to his waist, praying the undertow will not drag him out to sea, the current won't pull him along the shoreline, overpowering his questionable swimming. First arms are lowered to the water. It's freezing. All the questions of courage and what it is to be a man have been asked. Wasn't he once a great swimmer? Wasn't I once a great lover? Don't go in the water.

I turned to my right and opened the door. Pitch-black. I couldn't see my hand in front of my face. It took courage to move forward. My state of mind was purely that of a moron proving the outer limits of idiocy. Each of my feet sinking into the deep carpeting, my right arm, certain that I was going to walk into the wall, extended in front of me.

Crash! I walked straight into the wall. The pain was dull. My mind was spinning while I waited for the pain to run its course. My nose was bleeding. The door shut behind me with a bang like a strong breeze had slammed it closed. If I wanted out then, I could have reversed my tracks, felt the wall and opened the door. But I didn't have time to make any such decision. A presence in that room pulled my attention to it.

Anyway, I spoke softly.

"Radiance . . . is that you?" No answer, as I expected. Footsteps but no response. I couldn't detect whether they were coming toward me or walking from the far side of the room to another place equally distant from where I stood. Then it was scurrying, like the sound of a rake sweeping dried, fall leaves into a heap. Over and over again came that same noise, not moving toward or away from me. Both of my hands were against the wall now, my skin shivering from what felt like a coat of freezing slime. My heart was throbbing, although nothing was visible except blackness. I refused to move, waiting for anything to be revealed. Nothing. Dead silence overcame all the movement I'd blindly witnessed. Suddenly, I felt those winds again, enveloping me. I tried to move. It was impossible, impaled by the invisible.

Still, I couldn't see anything; I was hearing sounds and feeling a strong wind, yes. Goddamnit, it was windy in a bedroom on Park Avenue. What time was it? It must have been late; I'd daydreamed back in the hallway longer than a couple of hours. Fear erased my will to escape—there was no way out. The drapes were drawn.

Then the sounds came—a deafening frequency, approaching and fading. Ten, twenty, thirty high-pitched feedbacks, the wind was more intense. The pressure on my ears, my body, was unbearable. I discovered the depth of a will to live I never knew I possessed. It would've taken a greater effort that night to kill me. Perhaps they knew that, too, knew the line between life and death. I sensed that the objective of the torment wasn't to kill me but to push me to the edge, make me a prisoner in an apartment where evil was the dish de jour. Radiance went out, procured the victim and turned him over to Otis for further consideration. I'd followed the plan like a ballroom dance lesson at Arthur Murray, putting my feet in all the places.

What the hell could they want with me? What good could I do to her? The wind and the sounds stopped simultaneously, the propellers had turned their last revolution. Was I back at the line of scrimmage?

It was her bed.

I fell forward, weary, not quite mortally wounded. What a miracle that I recall what happened. I don't know how long I lay there but I was too deranged to sleep.

The quiet was brilliant, filled with sonic terror. It did not matter; I didn't have the strength to lift myself from the bed. Curious no longer, I just wanted out. Whatever was happening, I chose returning to my mind-numbing lawyer's life, talk to my clients, sit in my swivel chair until hell froze over. The lessons of romance plus adventure were taught to me. Now it was too late; I couldn't escape and in this darkness I had no idea of what I'd be running toward or away from.

At that second, I heard gurgling, I saw ripples sucked down a drain. Not once did I think about how we met, that dumb discussion before the rain, of the proper way to bring up children.

After all, I did see her this morning in bed, beautiful as could be, harmless as could be sleeping. If there was a monstrosity there, I never saw it through the veil of night. I had to dwell on the belief that she also didn't know a thing about what was occurring, that she had no responsibility for the damage being done to me.

Then I heard the goddamn beeping coming at me with the sound of a crashing plane's emergency alarm propelled at me, the sole passenger.

"Beep, beep, beep, beep . . ." The winds lifting me, then gently placing me down on the bed as if I were her breakfast tray, then throwing me back against the headboard. Then my clothes were ripped, clawed, torn, yanked from me. I was vandalized, naked without a hand touching me or contact from the whatever, leaving fresh meat for any purpose.

So now I waited. Yes, terror! I was never promised a quiet death in a respectable nursing home. But I didn't want to experience the sordid end of my most horrible nightmares, eaten by gargantuan flies, snagged in the web of cantaloupe-size spiders, waiting to be preyed upon by dripping wet lizards. All of those ends were lurking in that bleakness. The black room. And there it was again, the damnable flapping, like flags unfurling in a typhoon, a carpet beaten with a club. It came straight for me . . . the beeping screaming, thick as syrup, sounds flooding, drowning my eyes and ears, every pore. Christ, I was beyond double lifetimes, double deaths. The claws of this beast uprooting my flesh, ripping my nipples, butchering my body, next in line at the abattoir. Fingernails digging, mangling me into an animal discarded on the roadside. I was eaten like filet mignon in a five-star, but fucking some creature at the same time. The monstrosity was satisfying its urgent sexual needs. I could feel liquid all over me as if wrung from a sponge and wiped over me like soap. Shit, I was nothing but a piece of skin. The beeping growing drunkenly louder, louder, goddamn loud white noise, blasting my ears. My body was a devoured carcass, torn from limb to vein, organ to marrow, mashed, crushed, pulverized, ground into nothing. Every curdling scream, screech, yell, call for help, plea in agony, need was lost. The biting, the whirring, the flapping, the chomping of this animal was total consumption. I was finished. . . . I was at the entrance of my last moments. I was at Violet Avenue.

CHAPTER XI

I am so tired I don't think I'll ever be able to go out. I am weak. I may have leukemia, mononucleosis, warm air blown through my body like a brown paper shopping bag. Yet I am taking all of it calmly; I can't give a damn. No strength, no will . . . a glass of water awaiting evaporation. I'll start watching television, see the news. I must keep myself informed, straight, feel all the strife of what this hotel room means. But this is my home. I will try to forget the last thing I recall, then blissful sleep. What is the last thing I recall? A sensation, my mind was filled with that room. These walls breathe, coming closer and then exhaling like an accordion. Finally, my head is emptied.

I can't find a sleeping position. My arm under my head, my legs crossed and uncrossed, now on my stomach. All my positions have expired like the date on an old can of beef stew. Now I have started to think, exactly what I didn't want to do. I have stirred up a refrigerator loaded with midnight snacks; I am not going to dream those nightmares, fighting the wars of all countries, falling from cliffs, trapped in flooded caves, losing every love affair, a hermit in this room. Instead I will plan my escape. It will require a total commitment to sanity.

I have had another nervous breakdown, *une crise de nerfs*.

The last time was years before I met Radiance Tempest. One day I simply got out of bed and walked right onto a fire escape inside my bedroom. There was no fire and no escape. This time I knew it would not go away. It was here permanently. It would get worse over the next few months and then stay that way. In the earlier days I cured these attacks with repression. I could cover it over with good old faux strength. But how does one become strong when at one o'clock everything is OK, things are in their proper places, coat in the closet, iced tea in the fridge. Twenty-four hours later the clock says it ran out of time and the little hand is crooked. My mind is a vegetable garden. All the plants—thousands of them with my face—are staring at me.

So many feelings were racing around and I knew only one thing for certain . . . I had no control; it had been taken from me. There were no clothes to wear in the closet where I dressed. No strength in my arms. There was no room to understand whether or not it was a good thing. The past was replacing the present, wiping out time. A whole new way of living each horrible event replayed for me, each impression on the tip of a pointed metal bristle of a wire brush, scrubbing the inside of my head. Shit! The past was entirely too painful for me.

I became a lawyer because no one would say that was bad, even though I know better now. I won, I lost, I won, I lost and that math totaled a career. Of course I would have chosen this profession if I'd been given an engraved gold pocket watch, a three-piece suit, and a bum leg to start. Suits don't fit me; I hate time, and I have two good legs so . . . I'll never be Robert Taylor representing the Mafia in "Party Girl"—my childhood fantasy which led me by the nose through law school, the bar exam and all the cursed events since. Don't watch television, you'll be sorry. I'm afraid I'll be a lawyer again and again and again.

So, I didn't become a disciple of that line of overweight, gray-haired, rosy-cheeked attorneys retained for one million dollars by a widowed Palm Beach murderess to acquit her.

But when I went crazy, I focused on important things like, should I wear wool or cotton? I just didn't know. Decisions, the first one of every day, is what to wear; I was stuck at the closet door. The mind broken apart like a child's toy, faltering like an errant lawn mower plowing up dirt and rocks, all this anguish at the closet. After standing there full of indecision I dropped to my knees, cried, fell asleep, and I knew I had to get help.

The phone. Dial a number, seek a friend's recommendation.

"Here lies Brane, he died in the nude trying to decide what to wear."

That first time I called Blake. I remembered what he said to me years ago when he was having trouble keeping a grip. He told me he'd been to see a doctor and was being honest with someone on a professional level because he went to a pre-appointed place at a pre-appointed time. The idea and organization of a schedule to confer with a shrink set him back on the road to sanity. I'd never forgotten that, although when he told me about it I didn't think I'd ever need to see a doctor right now.

As I was trying to stand straight up in my little room, I thought about what I would do if Blake weren't home. I couldn't think of anyone else to turn to and, whenever I am in a crisis, I can't recall who my friends are.

But I was lucky, he was just leaving the house. It was about nine-thirty and he said to me, "I know how you feel, try to stay on top of it. I'll call Sam for you, Sam will take care of you."

"Blake, I realize this sounds stupid, but I have to see him right away, I'm flipping, and I can't stop it. "

"I'll call him and call you right back," he answered and hung up. No less than a minute went by, and the phone rang.

"Hello, is this Brane?" His voice was filtered through the nose.

"Yes." I knew it was the shrink; it was the soothing, sonorous quality that is so often used for clients in distress.

"If it is an emergency, I can see you tomorrow afternoon at three o'clock." He was friendly, calming, acting like he wasn't a doctor and he was being cool, not mentioning Blake.

"No, Doctor, I don't think I can wait that long," I said out of my wild hysteria. "I would like to see you this afternoon at one. Is that possible? "

"I don't know. I'd have to switch some things around, sounds unlikely. Can I phone you back in a little while?"

"What's a little while?" I hate indefinite measurement, I wanted a precise time.

"Oh, it's like that!"

"Yes, what's a little while?" I demanded.

"Twenty minutes."

"Too long! "

"Maybe I am not the right doctor for you."

"I have to get started with someone. I must talk to someone; I can't go on this way for more than another five or six minutes."

"OK, I'll call you back as soon as I find out. It shouldn't be more than a few minutes."

"OK"

For the next forty-five minutes he didn't ring back, and I couldn't pick up the phone to call anyone else. I was so afraid he'd accidentally go to voice mail. The delay made me crazier at first; I didn't know what to do. My heart started fluttering, skipping beats, and I broke into a cold sweat. I was counting seconds; soon I would be suicidal. In the process I began to gain strength. Out of adversity comes power. How weak could I become; how dependent should I be on a fucking doctor anyway? Hadn't I existed all my life without some M.D. talking to me about how I should do this or that, what I did wrong?

Finally, the independent bastard called me back.

"I can see you this afternoon at three-thirty." I could tell he was writing in his appointment book.

"Doc, I think I'll try to go it alone for a few days. I feel like I should rely on some of the small strength I have and see if I can make it. I don't want to be this reliant." Where the fuck did that burst of fortitude come from?

"I understand, I think that's a good idea. How about Friday at four-thirty?"

"Good. I'll see you then."

When the call was over, I didn't believe what I'd done in desperation and what I had done because I was not desperate.

Now I can't remember what I did during that time from Wednesday morning (when I was walking on the fire escape running from the foot of my bed into the wild blue yonder) to Friday, except I think I went to work and struggled around the office.

At that time, I didn't have access to my secretary, so there were no witnesses to the madness. But around three that Friday I left to see the doctor. I was wearing a pair of blue velvet pants and carrying a pair of jeans in my briefcase in case I freaked on the way and had to change. I wasn't certain about what was the right thing to say, wear, watch, or listen.

His office was in an apartment building in the West Nineties on the fifth floor. No elevator, just a fucking climb. He had a waiting room full of magazines: car racing, fashion, housekeeping, Newsweek—a veritable bunch of shit one was forced to read to kill time. No matter when patients arrived, he'd make them wait. The waiting room was windowless, a prison cell with a cheap Pakistani runner, Danish Modern furniture and black, spindle-back chairs—reminders of just how I went off my rocker.

I was the only one there, maybe I was his only patient. I read and I read and I read. The room had three doors leading from it like a set on a TV quiz show. It was clear Sam shared the rented space with two other shrinks.

A door pushed open as I was finishing a Time article in "The Law" section about a mass murder in a Midwestern town.

The doctor didn't introduce himself, but he shook my hand; one of his fingers was missing and I sensed a lot more wasn't there. We went down a narrow hallway to his office, a tiny room with a brown leather armchair, a matching hassock for the doc, and I was to sit on a small couch opposite.

First, we got the financial stuff out of the way—how much per visit; I agreed to the fee and there were no problems just then. The first one came when he explained to me that an hour was not an hour but forty-five minutes. I began to legally argue that point, but I told myself to screw it, I needed the attention fast. There was dead silence. I realized I was supposed to speak—to talk about my problems. Then I had to seriously assess the exact problems to be fixed and, if they were fixed, would that bring back my sanity or was I just crazy and that state of mind had nothing to do with the problems. Time was passing, the clipped hour was nearly over, so for the sake of economy I jabbered on and on about women, law, mixing it all with sparse witticisms about growing up, historical tidbits, a few original jokes and, last but not least, I presented him with several moments of pure sadness and despair. I don't know whether I did that because any of it was true or because I thought I should get my money's worth. I hate being taken for a ride by another professional.

This process of seeing and talking to a figure called a psychiatrist went on between me and Sam for about six months; once or twice a week I would leave my hotel room or my office and go uptown for horizontal reasons. He had me laying on that couch, yakking my ass off. Most of those days, I recall, I did not have anything to say, and my condition was not improving. Sam never said much beyond "Hello" when I entered and the ensuing, purposeless silence would be broken by Sam. He pretended to take notes.

"So, Brane, how has the week been?" Then, of course, I would begin to talk about anything that came into my head and things that didn't enter that space at all.

So, one day I said to him, "Doctor, enough time has passed, and I don't feel we are getting anywhere."

"It takes time," he answered and that was a lot for him to say. Whenever something isn't working the service provider always says, "It takes time," because they charge by the hour.

"I visit you here, then when I leave, I forget everything, despite the attempts I make to remember what you made me say and what you said. You never tell me anything except that I must break the cycles that I have created for myself and how these cycles relate to my mother and father. All I see are these motorcycles racing in concentric circles around the inside of a metal pot, saddlebags loaded with problems, and me stepping up with a scythe trying to break or cut the Harley-Davidson.

"In the past six months that's about all you've made me think about. I walk the streets, I practice law, go to sleep, brush my teeth, saying to myself "I must break these cycles," and yet every time I anticipate something bad happening or can't cope with things, I do a somersault and wind up on Violet Avenue in Room Thirty-one at The Hotel Randolphe. That's the only decent defense I have left. What's tearing me apart is that every tiny thing is getting around or through the defenses and I have to deal with everything I've shut out since I was a kid being picked on by other boys in the schoolyard. I am attacked from all sides by years of reality I pushed out of the way. That's why I deal with myself in such a destructive manner, because I have gotten used to the pain and I like what happens to me when I overcome it. If I eliminate those bad things from my life, my existence will wind down into a total bore."

He looked at me across the top of his notepad, smiling.

"The problem is that when I listen to you, Brane, I don't know whether to laugh or cry. The stories you tell are so full of humor but sad. Just when I think you are in deep pain you make me laugh." I was certain his face had shrunk into the shape of rotted peach.

"What I recommend is that you go through analysis. It's five times a week, a serious commitment. Think it over. There seem to be problems which are so deeply rooted that I will even see you on Saturdays." The nectar was leaking down to his neck.

He sounded like he was offering a discount deal or telling himself that he personally needed to see me five times a week. I was sold, sucked into the Freud game, buying into his pyramid or Ponzi scheme. A package deal; now the exterminator was coming every day and I was to be debugged.

"I have a place in the country. . . . It is right down Violet Avenue," I thought I heard him say. "You can drive there. It's an old refectory, a retreat. It's called The Citadel. For years I have had it. Very few people know about my little secret resting place, which happens to be longer, wider and higher than Buckingham Palace."

There was no reason to resist seeing him there. After all, wouldn't it be fantastic to see a psychiatrist in the countryside for a consultation rather than in a therapy cubicle on the West Side?

I drove up to The Citadel on the first Saturday. I didn't consider the implications of talking to a doctor five days out of seven a week. I only thought this miracle man was going to stitch my mind together even though he hadn't done me any good up to now.

I drove to the driveway entrance. It was wide, and it twisted and turned right to the front doors. The doctor wasn't kidding. The place was a monstrosity, an institution, complete with its own contiguous church. Across the lawn opposite the front door was a tower, where, he told me that the New York FBI office broadcasts and receives all of their messages. I believed him. It often occurred to me, who was crazy, me or the doctor? But I was on my way to get help because he was the doctor; I was trusting I could be cured in the head and survive. The thought that I'd be cured was nutritious.

His wife's car was parked. He once said that she had a Fiat with Nova Scotia plates. Two carved, unpainted oak doors with knuckle-shaped knockers awaited me. Banging and banging the knockers didn't get a reaction. He had to be in there, I told myself.

My eyes flashed to the car, to the rooftop, scanned the windows, back to the door. Why the hell didn't he hear me? The building was huge; it was like screaming at city hall for the mayor. After ten minutes of frustration, I ran to the car and drove around to the rear. The driveway hooked into a delivery entrance, alongside a granite veranda. I got out of the car, leaving the door open, the radio broadcasting to the Bavarian woods' vista. There were five steps to the veranda. I yelled his name and it echoed off the building, bouncing into a cloud-filled day.

"Doctor, doctor, doctor, what am I going to do?" Again no response. I repeated myself, hands on my hips, standing with the cold wind in my face, contemplating the next moment. Some things I knew for certain, nailed down: The weather was overcast, I was driving a shiny sports car, I was dressed, I had a normal temperature, but that mind roaming around inside my head was ill.

From around the rear of the building a dark green pickup truck drove toward me at a great rate.

"Must be a handyman," I thought.

Sure enough, he was clad in dark green, including a baseball cap. A ten-year-old kid was with him. A moment later he was out of the truck, hustling toward me.

"What are you doing here? This is private property!" His Polish accent made me think I can handle the situation. I had a fucking country house and I'm half Polish!

I looked at his hardscrabble face, hairy eyebrows, coarsely combed, black-and-gray haircut. His short forearms were crossed like a railroad sign—he wasn't going to permit me to see the doc and that my treatment was in jeopardy. I stared into his eyes.

"I am trying to find the doctor," I muttered.

"What doctor?" He put the question to me as if I were about to be hit with a stretched elastic.

"The doctor, is there more than one?" I asked.

"The doctor, you know, the psychiatrist."

"There is no doctor here and who are you?"

Little did he know what an appropriate question that was. The reason for our accidental meeting was just that. I plodded on, although I just didn't have the mental strength to argue. I suggested that we drive around to the front of the building, where I'd seen the car.

"There's no need to argue. I'm a patient of the doctor's, he told me to come up today."

Now the confusion—the doctor would see patients on the weekends. Those Polish eyebrows twisted inward.

He repeated, "There is no doctor here! You must have the wrong house. . . . Get off the property!"

"Well, if there is no doctor here, whose car is parked in front?"

"I don't know." He stood there unimpressed with my question. "You must leave now; you have no right to be here!" His right hand became a barrier, pointing to the driveway.

Without a word, I turned the engine over, revved and rolled it past him in neutral, coasting in the direction of where he'd pointed. As soon as I was ten feet from him, I slammed the shift into first and roared around the side of the house back to the front door. In the rearview mirror I saw him hunched over the wheel, following on my heels.

I pulled in front of the Fiat, using it as a shield, and jumped out, ready for the unknown. My illness was exacerbated by this bastard who was ridiculously blocking me from seeing the one man I believed could save me. I needed allies, not someone treating me like a fugitive. As I stepped from the car and watched him angrily come for me, I wondered if the doctor had given me a line of bullshit and my insanity had dreamed up the whole thing about the car, his Nova Scotia plates, and this wasn't his house. Nothing made sense. Instantly I was putting my hands out and said, "Well, if there isn't any doctor here, whose car is that? He's got a Fiat, that's a Fiat, a blue one . . . and it has his license number. I know because I've seen him drive it in the city."

The caretaker stopped me again.

"No doctor here . . . look at his plate, it would say MD, that's the law in New York. Now get off the property before I do something you'll regret."

"It's his fucking wife's car. . . . His wife lives in Nova Scotia, that's why there's no M.D. plates."

Silence. He smiled, put his hand out dementedly. Talk about ipso flipso facto.

"All right . . . I'm Jules, I'll take you inside to see the doctor. You understand, so many people, kids, Sunday drivers, damn cowboys on motorcycles come up the driveway to see what's here, claiming they know who lives in this place. I have to be so careful. "

I reached out and shook his Velcro hand while my brain flopped over like Jell-O. Did I need this confrontation before seeing my shrink? He was the prick who was at fault, telling me to come here, run the caretaker's gantlet. Jules called out to his son.

"Come with us."

The kid smiled at me, like I was an old friend of his father's, and we went to the door. From his belt loop Jules unhooked the key. He turned the handle and we walked into a small vestibule leading to a door under a stained-glass transom of Jesus' crown of thorns dotted with ruby red eyes.

We walked to the elevator. Exit signs everywhere, I realized, because this place was an institution.

"What do you do for a living, sir?"

The one thing I prayed was I wouldn't have to talk to anyone except the doctor.

"I'm a lawyer," I answered feeling like a mildewed tablecloth slipped over an old picnic table. The lawyer. Now the boy was frightened of me, tugging the crease in his father's pants. The elevator doors opened. The grin on Jules' face widened as he pressed Three.

As we ascended, he laughed dismissively, "You mean apprentice to a lawyer!" His meaty fingers and dirt-caked nails pointed at me.

"No, I really am a lawyer."

"No."

"No, Jules . . . I am a lawyer . . . I look young, but you'd be surprised if I told you how long I've been suing people."

Shit, what difference did that make. I should have said I was a hanger salesman. Then would he have claimed, "No, you mean apprentice to a coat hanger salesman!"

The pain in the back of the neck, the radiating line down to my hand into my fingers—I could be a suffering octogenarian. One event bleeding into the next, no time for the slightest, smallest break from destruction. Jules opens his inquisition and embraces, crushes the tiny, valued jewels of my brain tissue that allowed me to drive for help. Now, in this metal box I have to talk to this fucker.

I should've stopped before at a local diner, ordered breakfast just to see a standard image: sausage, eggs, home fries and slices of buttered toast on a plate, a brimming cup of black coffee, a white napkin, a New York City tabloid full of violence, gossip, same-sex marriage and politics would bring me back to sanity.

But the service is bad in this diner; the waitress' uniform is dirty, the counter is shellacked molasses, maple syrup, eggs Benedict, stale bread crumbs and corn bread morsels, customers yakking in busybody sentences and the manager won't turn down Bill Haley and the Comets' "Rock Around the Clock."

The bastard cashier wants me to pay for this; I didn't eat anything. They should pay me for patronizing this shit hole; they're intensifying my breakdown with their roadside retching station.

Filthy restaurant proprietors report here to the courtyard and admit you poisoned us with your unsanitary bathrooms, your filthy floors, your fly-infested tomato soup, corroded spoons, your pink lips uttering pedantic political propaganda. Piss on you. Furthermore, the same to you, you lame bastard Jules for your fucked-up interrogation of a man as sick as I, your sixth-grade schooling. I was only coming to see my doctor and the property rights of man have been expanded to the whole world. Don't you know about history? There is no private property. Everyone has a doctor!

Anyhow, the elevator thumped to the third floor, rattling us like ice cubes in a cocktail tumbler, the door slides open, we march, march, march—father, son escort me to the doctor, who has promised me tranquility, peace from the invaders.

The darkened hallway walls were freshly painted. As we walked along the corridor, I noticed many empty bedrooms with sloped ceilings and dormer windows.

We arrived at the last door. A tiny black plastic nameplate on the door read Dr. Sam Delzio, Room 31. That was familiar.

Without asking Jules, I tapped on the door. No answer.

"I know he's in there, knock again . . . but you'd better be his patient or I'm really in for it," Jules whispered, pointing at the door.

I rapped on the door.

"Doc, it's me, Brane, are you in there?

Minutes passed and finally the door flew open. The doctor came at me with outstretched arms. His Castro beard irritated my neck. He furiously grabbed and unjustifiably hugged me tightly. I could hardly breathe.

"This is my patient . . . Brane." He proudly announced. Am I his only patient? The voice superficially boasting. A bleach-blonde, blue-eyed, short-legged girl stood behind him, looking haggard. She climbed onto the bed.

"My dear Brane, I didn't think you were going to show up." Those arms were still around me.

"Jules, you can leave now." Jules placed his hand on his son's shoulders and left.

The doctor looking very unstable, called me "Dahling" and slammed the door. He was wearing a sea captain's hat and a navy-blue blazer. The crest of the 1976 U.S. Olympic team was sewn onto the pocket. The bastard was kite high. The ship was caught in a huge storm, and he was shuffling from port to starboard. A vial of coke was next to several lines on a tray, along with a Zip-loc bag of pot on a narrow table at the foot of the bed.

"My boy," he said, his black eyes bulging, "my treatment tools, roll yourself a J, snort a tad of coke and take a gander out the window. The vista. Better view than from any fucking castle in Austria, Germany, Switzerland, anyplace. You know I'm a baron but they don't have titles in this fucked-up country."

He rolled a joint and vacuumed two lines, while I acquiesced that he was a real baron, it was the eighth century and we were safe here from a barbarian attack.

The blonde girl who I assumed was a baroness moved backward on the bed, said she was afraid of a lizard, but she and her fear were ignored. The doctor's right arm was around my shoulder, we could have been father and son gazing at the view. He acted like a conqueror showing off his conquests.

The coke froze my nostrils and throat. I was breathing through my head. The girl inched her way up the bed, perhaps another lizard slithered in her direction. I watched her and understood she was a patient cum girlfriend.

"Doc, I must talk to you, what we spoke about earlier in the week, about going through analysis. You asked me to come up here. Today was wicked, wicked, wicked, I can't take it."

I didn't know in the moment if I was nuts because I was stoned or was I in my everyday crazy. My memory was billowing, blowing back and forth like being in love with two women. A part of me cried out for shrinking; after all, I came for that and I had an appointment. This little cry for help squeaked from my stoned, dulled, anesthetized body.

"But Doctor, we had an appointment today. You fucking promised. This morning, like six months ago, I woke up, walked out on a fire escape in my bedroom. . . . There is no fire escape there, and also the giant garden, double-headed plants growing, each head was mine making decisions. I'm not well. Let's talk. Is there a couch?"

The girl's inching now put her back against the headboard. She screamed, "I'm going to be crucified."

Look bitch, it's my turn. What I was there for was an assessment of my worth: Was I staying alive or what? He had to come forth in his well-trained Harvard head and recommend "the treatment." Would he speak to me about my illness? No. I was beginning to wish that Jules didn't go. Maybe he could treat me more professionally than this Sam doc.

At the point when he sensed that he'd have to deal with the severity of my condition, he turned and stared at me as if I had trespassed.

"Come on outside."

So, I walked across the room past the baroness now flattened against the headboard like a slice of Kraft American cheese. He pulled at the door and stared at me.

"Let's go, I want to show you this place," he said.

I wanted my appointment, not a grand tour. He complained, "What the hell did you come over here for? Don't you see I am with someone!"

"We have an appointment. I am paying you. "

"But I am with a girl."

"How was I supposed to know?"

"You can see, can't you?"

"You opened the door, didn't you?" I am yelling in a whisper.

"So, what, you, you . . . must leave soon!"

"But I must first talk to you . . . I am really sick, especially today."

"You must leave, you are freaking her out . . . and I am getting depressed listening to you. You are ruining my afternoon!"

"You told me to come, to tell you my problems which have reached epic heights, code red! You are my goddamn doctor, remember?" He ignored me.

"Come on with me, I want to show you the church and the vestry. "

At the end of the corridor, a doorway opened onto a balcony with two chairs apparently for priests to view the service. The church seats about a thousand worshipers, complete with confessionals in locations alongside the pews. He showed me around the altar and the portraits of Christ done in the Fifties. There was a vestry, a chapel, and rooms for the clergy.

"There are over one hundred and fifty rooms here: classrooms, bedrooms for the staff, bathrooms, kitchens, sitting rooms, corridors and corridors. Some people call it a hotel."

That sounded familiar. We went to the boiler room, he wanted to show me the furnaces,

"Look here, they are the size they use on battleships," he proudly pointed out like a naval officer.

We walked and talked about every detail of the building and not a word about me and my eroding life. I couldn't shut him up.

"Do you believe this place? I am a baron, I am a baron," he raved after each room. I was suddenly understanding that everything was going to be all right. I could never be as crazy as he was and I got it—he was showing me the outer limits of insanity and I was normal. This was his version of an appointment.

After the tour we returned to his room.

"Why don't you move in?" he shouted and sat back on the bed, throwing his arms around her. Without waiting for an answer, he kissed her neck and her breasts, grunting like a hog.

He looked up at me for approval.

"The Baroness has to be back soon; she has two children to take care of and she can't listen to your problems, that's what I am here for. What's wrong, pal? Five times a week I told you, analysis, anal this, anal that, get it, but we can't start on a Saturday, not this Saturday or any Saturday soon. Plus, she has to be back with her kids."

I got up to leave.

"Wait, I'll walk you downstairs," he offered, continuing to rave about being a baron again until we reached the foyer, then he went quiet. I faced him.

"Doc, has anything like this ever happened to you?"

"Yes, several times."

"When?"

The light in the foyer dimmed, he pushed the door open and moved outside. His lips turned inward. Clearly, he didn't want to answer me.

"When?" I asked again.

"When . . . when I realized what I wanted in life was never going to be."

I left the doctor standing at the top of the steps in front of his institution, pulling the brim of his captain's hat down, turning his back to me.

The experience did me a great deal of good. I understood why he was in pain, bad choices. By comparison I could never reach the height of his fuckedupness.

What the hell did I do about this breakdown? I stayed in her godforsaken Room Thirty-one after checking back into the Randolphe. It is obvious that I was not fit to go out and be with people. Is that why I keep myself holed up here in a hotel, like the night porter? Definitely not, I would've liked to have gone outside. First, I'd take a shower, wash my hair and put on a clean shirt . . . a white one . . . not like this rag I've been wearing; I've got some clean cotton pants that fit well and I haven't worn them in a long time. Yes, those clothes will fit and feel right. The street will be an easier place to walk if I am comfortable. So, I must be getting self-conscious; why shouldn't I be? Maybe if there weren't so damn many mirrors in her apartment, I wouldn't be staring at myself so often. All of it expected; I can't be too hard on myself . . . after a night like this I have to at least see if I still appear to be human.

Here I am in her bedroom. Son of a bitch, not a scratch. . . . There must be welts all over my back, the skin on the arms and legs must have been gouged. I must have been dead. The mirror lies. No, it is the truth. As I am looking myself over I see that there isn't a scratch . . . not even the ones on my face from our first date. And would someone please tell me how long I've been wasting away in this bathroom, examining these nonexistent wounds, recounting the unproven horrors of this acquaintance, Ms. Radiance Tempest. OK, get it straight! We are in the apartment. My breakdown is over! It was just another uneventful night with Radiance.

Daylight! It must be early morning; the light isn't strong enough to be later. Why does that anger me? Is this the frustration from adventure? I would be suffering without Ms. Tempest in my life. I am the spectator. How long will I stay in this room? There she is. I'm going to get her. Impossible, she's asleep again. The covers, red wool resting on her upturned shoulder like rolling tumbleweed. The innocence filling the space between my eyes, and her curled body nestled into the unconscious while I am trapped investigating the previous night, which she couldn't know a thing about. Look at her! I am the crazy one. This is no different from when I was a child, trying to plead to my parents that I am right, knowing all the time I would feel better being wrong, being put in my proper place. Radiance will do it.

This day seems to be exactly like the last. But now I am armed or rather I have made preparations because I won't have to contend with Otis. He'll never get loose, so I can go into the kitchen and make my own coffee. No, today is another day, the first moments of my new life. There she is, my girl, sweet, innocent . . . my lover. She has not done me any harm. The world and I see that I am whole and intact. No, last night was just a nightmare in a shower of evil I inflicted upon myself. There is no reason to tell her about my doctor's appointment. Would she understand?

The sun is out, bright, a carved yellow banana, and I am going out to get a tan, put on a light blue button-down shirt tapered at the waist so I can make my appearance debonair. When she awakens and regards me as her lover she'll know we are totally correct for one another. Beige pants. Furthermore, I do know how to dress properly, no problems around the closet. Brown-and-white shoes that are pointed and speckled with tiny holes like the old days. I even have a pair of black, silk ankle-high socks and a narrow, red tie. Can I miss in that costume? I am just a guy looking for a mate.

Her attraction to me is really all that is important because I have to admit I cannot leave her; I'll do anything to keep it this way. The fragrance, which some would consider a hideous sickness that I have contracted, is merely love of another being. The knowledge I possess of how I can pass over a repugnant a human form because I'm in a love story. I am in love with her. What else could it be that would keep me on these premises? But I am trying to sort out the parts of her I love, since I have been around her only inconsistently and haven't been side by side with her, except for the exits from the bed I've made two mornings in a row. I'll wake her and get this whole ordeal straight. No, I'd better not do that. I'm the man, she has to come to me. For all this time I waited I want some satisfaction.

CHAPTER XII

Later that morning I grew hungry and went to the kitchen. Where I obtained the power to leave her, I will never know; nevertheless, I was able to do it. Again, silently I moved over the bedroom carpeting and turned the doorknob as if it were a bank vault combination lock. Now I recall how much I feared her. There was Otis; he hadn't stirred. The smack on the head had really bulged, melon-like in the middle of his forehead. The pain in his arms and legs from being tied all night must have been excruciating. I wanted to see him grimace, I needed to satisfy every bit of sadism in me they had instigated. Now I was the animal, that survived

The door to the kitchen was ajar. An old-fashioned wood burning stove was at one end. Pots and pans were on each burner, and they looked used. The floor was slate. The room reminded me of what Angelo had said about her, fucking weird. A draft blew through the kitchen, making me shiver.

About ten feet to the left of the stove there was a yellow ice box. It had four doors with stainless steel handles. Next to it were glass cabinets filled with dishes that my grandmother would have thrown out. They were wood and metal and there were wooden drinking mugs. I opened the cabinet and took one in my hand, turned it around. On the back was an inlaid jade piece with the face of a woman with bat features. I set it down and lit a cigarette. The intrigue was bottomless. One by one I placed each of the mugs down on the counter. They all had the same jade piece, clean as if they'd been washed that morning. I blew smoke rings and played Detective Nowhere.

I rubbed the butt out and placed the mugs back. Again, a chill went through my body and I imagined hearing wind chimes hanging on the porch of a wind-swept oceanfront cottage. Then I looked for coffee. My head was beginning to spin, and I felt a splitting headache erupting. Without thinking, I pulled open a cabinet door. The shelves were stacked with Mason jars full of what appeared to be coconut flakes or spices. I began to shut the door but instead I reached in, took one of the jars down, accidentally dropping it. The contents scattered all over the stone floor. Hundreds of moths, loose antennae, the wings attached like they'd been caught with a net and died moments later, beetles, spiders and last but not least a black widow. Each one was intact, as though they were used for an entomology class. Their insect enmity for mankind stared at me from their deadened bodies. I thought they were moving, waking, talking to me. I felt them squealing, singing some shrill thin sound about Radiance. My arms were swollen with goose bumps, like hairs on a frightened cat's back. I straightened up and slowly peered into the cabinet. More bottled house flies, mosquitoes, insects of every strain. Then I ripped open the other cabinets. Full of the same stuff. I ran to the door and shoved it open. Otis was standing there. I bounced off his bare chest.

"Sir," his mouth yawned, "I asked you not to go into the kitchen. Ms. Tempest only allows me in there." The fright from what I'd just seen, on top of running into him, was too much. I screamed like I imagine a woman does when she's being raped. His hands pressed at my neck, indenting the Adam's apple to meet my spinal cord. Like a valve being shut, the scream died and became a death gasp. There was nothing I could do. I thought my head was going to burst from the force. I must have passed out again or died. The next thing I remember was waking up on that couch with a stiff neck.

My eyelids lifted and I could see the blurred outline of the same tray on which I was served that spiked coffee two days ago. It was steaming; the aroma of coffee entered my nose. The idea of once more being alive was fantastic. Surely, he could have killed me; I'd offered no resistance.

"Good morning, Brane." I recognized her voice. It had that same sweet phone quality.

"Did you sleep well?" The sound was one hundred percent correct and innocent. "Yes," I meekly groaned, agreeing with all the surroundings.

Suddenly the room was darkened; again I couldn't see a thing or detect where the voice was originating. My eyes were smarting like smoke was being blown at me or a gas was sprayed in the room. I rubbed my face and eyes trying to see anything at all. That was useless. The atmosphere was the same as those times I was in her room before the onslaughts. But by now I was tired of being frightened. I figured out that my fear derived from anticipating the stroke of death. They weren't going to kill me, that was evident, because they would have iced me last night. Yet there was no reason to keep me alive other than entertainment purposes. The self-induced torture I had endured before I ever ran into Radiance was much less severe as anything she and her crew put me through. But I was tenacious. Then she was standing right next to me in her Ethiopian wedding dress. That fucking garment.

"Brane," her tone bellowing down at me, "you know I was thinking about us." Us, us, us echoing as if we were surrounded by canyons. I like you so much. . . . We can have a wonderful relationship."

Damnit, she was acting like Muriel. The lights went on. Her right hand stroked her chin as if she had a beard, maybe a wad of Spanish moss. Silence. I didn't respond, waiting for her to commit herself to the truth, the goddamn facts of what happened, to explain everything including Otis, who was nowhere to be seen.

Seconds later, she said, "It is fantastic. I can't recall when I've been able to sleep so peacefully, just having my arms around you, knowing you're there in the same bed with me brings tranquility to my life. . . Usually I dream so much—horrible nightmares. I wake in the middle of the night crying because I am so alone, so damn isolated and desperate."

The smile on her face turned sour, hideous. Her teeth were long, the size of piano keys. Shit, she would have scared a shaman in the middle of a weird ritual. Her eyes drew toward the bridge of her nose. Were they trying to meet one another? Her chestnut-brown hair formed a point in the center of her forehead, triggering sharp sensations in my forearms and the back of my neck. She was a beautiful creep.

God, I was drifting back into her realm. How could I stop it? My brain started to grind; I had to hold off listening to her. I held my breath and pulled my ribs in to distract myself from being charmed by her but I saw her crossing her legs, sitting on the couch, pulling the red dress up to her thighs, exhaling, sexhaling showing me her wet vagina. She was coming on like a schoolgirl, and it was working.

"Are you listening to me?"

"Yes," I forced the word out, revealing the full extent of my resistance. "Yes," I repeated, fully aware of the trail I was being led down.

"What are you going to do today, go to your office? . . . You must have a lot of work to do." Wasn't that sarcastic? She didn't give a flying f if I went to an office or to a Ferris wheel.

Didn't she know I'd been hanging around this fucking apartment for two days waiting for her to get up, make an appearance? That I'd been tortured, been in a fistfight with her ignoramus manservant, had discovered her insect collection in the kitchen and, on top of it, had made love to a monstrosity, the chimera she turned into at night, or whatever was in that bedroom? I was about to approach her with all of it, have a complete confrontation. Then I looked at her and she gazed, yes, a romantic gaze which said she was kind, considerate and falling in love with me. That stopped me, I subverted all intentions of payback for the fright and emotional frustration on my side of the ledger.

"Yes." Giving in, I said one word.

"Yes, what?"

"Yes."

"What does that mean?"

"I must do some work today; I have meetings all day." I lied. I couldn't believe the entire idea. She and Otis letting me out to inform the world what went on here. It was too far-fetched. They'd never let me go; she had to be playing with me, giving me some ludicrous hope to hang onto before they ran me through the next gantlet. I sat back and brought the edge of the coffee to my lips but I didn't drink.

"Well, I am really going to miss you today. Do you think you could come back in the afternoon, and we could have tea together?"

The expression on her face was clear, sincere, as if she had no inkling of what I was thinking about her hell that rained down on me. I played along, aware I didn't know whether it was day or night. The office! What the f was that, computers, copying machine, some No. 2 pencils and a bill from the printer?

It seemed like Walpurgis Night to me. Then I began to feel fear again, just when I thought I had it beaten and brought down into a tiny compartment, where I could control it. Only now it was a fear of never seeing her again, never being afforded entrance into this fucking apartment again, never being able to feel as if I could wrap my arms around her deathly person, never being able to fulfill the depths of the tortured soul I lived within, never being able to climax with death. Yes, bastards, I wanted to be eaten alive, to be burned at the stake, glass rods broken inside my ass, stabbed in the heart, my head crushed between avalanching mountains, blown apart by grenades, crawled on by red ants, choked by octopus tentacles, injected by vats of morphine, drowned in alcohol and raided by every disease known to medicine.

She was at the hallway. They were setting me free. For the first time I saw how large her ears were, sticking up like Doberman's, peaked at the top, reddened at the edges.

We were hand in hand at the door. Radiance was kissing me, sticking her tongue into my mouth, licking my tongue. Her wiry body gyrating, dancing. My hands traced her back bones, finding her waist. I kissed her neck and hid in the darkness of her long hair, hoping for her to ask me to stay. There was no other place in the world I wanted to be. The way she smelled didn't bother me, that same dried, polluted odor with a faint overtone of lilac fragrance. I thought about kissing her neck and decided against any moves; I was afraid.

I was bombarded with images of everyone I knew—they were dead, covered in poison, victims of head-on collisions, drowned in oceans. How could I tell her my fears? But I was in love with her and isn't a lover supposed to listen? So, I pushed my deranged head further into her thick forest of hair, hoping I'd never have to open my eyes and face the world outside her door.

"I am stunned I could feel so strongly about you, incredible, this is magic, absolute magic," she whispered, blowing the words into my ear but pulling back from me. She went on, "You must leave for your office, you'll lose your clients."

"Yes, I am late, I'll phone you later." Wasn't that senseless? I didn't know whether it was morning or afternoon, light or dark, snowing or raining.

Her hand reached past me and opened the door to the hallway.

"OK, see you later."

She replied, "Have a nice day," as Otis had, just as if it were on a T-shirt, a yellow sun in the background with a jackass emoji smiling face. The door closed and I walked to the elevator, turning to see if she were watching me.

A doorman brought me to the lobby. Before I knew it, I was at the front door, about to step onto the sidewalk and freedom, and I hadn't even thought about whether it was day or night.

It was a great day, seventy degrees, clear as a parade day. I felt my neck for pain. Gone. I believed my mind had rolled down the crook of my right arm, off my fingertips and was in the air. There was traffic on Park Avenue and I couldn't figure out how to cross to the downtown side. I waited on the curb, trying to comprehend the first daylight and air I'd experienced in two days, that I was free to walk around the corner and even meet another woman.

No, I couldn't do that; all the boldness I felt was gone. Radiance had pulverized my confidence toward women. A naked, frightened feeling climbed around inside me just thinking about whether I should say hello or goodbye. I was drained of all the bullshit—telling women they were pretty, interesting, a knockout, sexy, fabulous, intriguing, asking if I could call or come over.

Clearly, I was lost, standing on the curb, trying to calculate when to cross over. The traffic signal was red; yes, I would wait for it to turn, I could do that. Green, there it was. I walked along, each step felt airy. Surely, I could've walked into a moving car, screamed obscenities, got on my knees and licked the pavement, complained about the food or sat on a manhole and cried for the death of Jesus.

Then suddenly a black limo drove toward me.

"No, this can't be true." I yelled, "The son of a bitch is running me down, going to kill me!" Who had I threatened? There were so many enemies I couldn't think fast enough. Hundreds of defendants in cases where I represented plaintiffs wanted vengeance.

Before it was too late, I flung myself to the curb, my outstretched hands touching the sidewalk. The driver barreled past and parked at the curb in front of a Park Avenue apartment house. My hands were raw, bleeding. I was shocked, not unlike a child in anguish after a bad fall. I ran to the driver's side, reached in, grabbed his neck and start choking him. Damn. It was Otis clad in a chauffeur's uniform. His head jerked back against the headrest, he struggled, his mouth hissing, then his nose blew snot over my knuckles. With his free hand, he pressed the window button. As the window was closing, I yanked my arm back, kicked the door. He didn't try to get out to stop me. People were lined up on the sidewalk, waiting for cabs and drivers, horrified, but no one tried to intervene.

I became calm, even though I was still shaking. I went to the trunk and beat the daylights out of it and finally I pounded the hood until it was bashed in. I stood in front of the car and hollered for him to get out, to "get the hell out and face me you motherfucker."

He didn't do anything. He wouldn't in broad daylight. I dusted myself off and walked to the other side of the street. I texted for an Uber. A few minutes later it arrived.

"Forty-sixth and Park on the near left corner."

The driver turned and asked, "What the hell went on here?"

"I don't know, they've been there all morning," I answered and pointed to the spectators

Damn it, that was crazy; was it Otis trying to run me down or my reaction to what I have been through? It could've been the lopsided state of New York I was in.

I knew my neighbor's watchdog when I was a kid who'd been run down a few times. After the last accident, he sat on the front lawn, on all fours, his front paws crossed, his mind gone. About every fifteen minutes he would see "the invisible thing" trespassing; he'd run to the edge of the lawn bark constantly until the neighbor shut it down. Fifteen minutes later that dog would be at the same place on the edge of the lawn, barking at another image. Finally, he had to be tied up in the house.

Now I was the dog. Did Otis really exist? Why didn't I ask her or tell her what happened while she slept? Why was he trying to kill me or was he?

I went up to my office and passed Pat.

"Hello, Brane. I didn't think you were coming in today, I hadn't heard from you."

"What do you mean? I come in every day."

I rapped the words off all four walls of the foyer as though I were trying to impress an eavesdropper. I am a lawyer that takes care of the business at hand, responsible, and I took the legal oath. After I settled behind my desk, propping the feet to one corner, I buzzed her, "Come in, please bring me the messages and the mail."

I was an actor who would examine scraps of paper and piece together a day's work: Calls would have to be made, bills would have to be paid, letters would need a response and deposits to the checking account were to be carried to the bank over on Madison Avenue. Shit, boring shit! I don't give a damn about any of those rules for making a living. What was saving me, sparing me from confronting the desert dry routine, was Radiance. As Pat walked toward me, my arms felt heavy, my neck fell forward, and in I went, tumbling into darkness.

Hours later, I found myself on the brown velvet couch where clients sat. My head was aching, my fucking body loaded with a late-night fatigue. Pat nurse-like, standing next to me, holding a glass of water. Her face was concerned, an expression that I could hardly attribute to anyone unless they were being paid. The pendulum of time had swung to deep, intractable emotion and I no longer wanted to create any activity out of the formless mold of existence except to be with the wrong woman. I thought about standing. Impossible, the idea slid backward like a dump truck unloaded. My shoulders were pinned, and I drew closer to death than life. Pat walked to the windows nervously watered some ficus plants, separated a cluster of leaves and looked at the city's skyline.

There was the image I had of myself as a kid, gazing at the largest city in the world, knowing, sagacious, contemplative; I'd conquer the metropolis, surmount NYC.

She didn't know what to do.

"Brane, I must phone a physician. You're more ill than you know. Your face is beet red, you must have a fever and I hate to say this to you . . . you look like death warmed over!"

"No, not that."

"Does that mean you refuse to see a doctor?" she asked angrily.

"Yes," I groaned.

The fever grew. I was burning up and I had to get my clothes off.

"I'm on fire." She rushed from the window, untied my shoes, my sweaty socks and tugged at the trousers until I was lying on the couch in my shirt and underwear. Well, there was my image I earned instead of what I aspired to—struggling with a malaria-like fever, being tended to by a secretary, an unidentifiable malady threatening to terminate a law career. Pain flew at me from every angle; my back felt split by an ax, my abdomen punched by a steel fist, my legs immovable and my head screeching like a car skidding on concrete.

"This is ludicrous," Pat shouted, "you've got to let me call a doctor. . . . My father knows doctors . . . at least let me call him." She was on the edge of tears, frightened.

"Please, please, Brane, do it for your own sake."

"No, don't call anyone, I'll be all right . . . I'll call an Uber, get me an ice pack; I'm getting dressed, going home," I insisted.

Sure, I can take care of myself, I'm going down Violet Avenue. I've done it for years. Just take a look around this pigpen. So, what if I never pick up what's on the floor? The one thing I should do is wash out that rubber trash container in the kitchen. I threw out those lobster tails I got from the hotel kitchen.

I long for those normal days when I could be composed, relishing the soft ideal of boredom. Now that I have time, I think I'll take a few of the pictures down and I'll hang my collection. There are Rodin prints I had stashed away from Paris. I have access to information. That means I can find it faster. I am a schooled student, a researcher of facts about life, a creator of conversation, an initiator of innovative ideas, thoughts that'll make people go home and talk about me, like he knows about vacuum cleaners; I know how to change the bag. If someone comes over, I can show them and we fold the clothes in the chest of drawers. They can take the TV out to be repaired.

Just like me, I have overstayed my time in this hotel flat; I wish they'd come, tow me out of here. I can't do it myself, trawl to the door. I need someone's help; someone has to hear what's been going on in here. That's very possible, the walls are so damn thin. It's not a First World War building; it's not all concrete. I can hear my neighbors, they can hear me, though no one ever told me to turn down the stereo or stop walking back and forth at

three in the morning. I wished they had, I could have used the company—
any face peering into my life I left behind and the one I am pacing through.
Anything, let the phone ring, wake me into a dimension where I can feel
anticipation for the next clean, bristling breath of cold air. Create a kid's
enthusiasm inside me so I can run outside, my winter coat flying in the wind,
watching a skywriter compose that everything up to now was beautiful.

No, this is just a room for rent where I occupy my time and their space,
and I can't get anyone to step forward and explain it to me. I don't think for
an instant in Brane's brain that I don't want contact! I do. Yes, I have said
too much.

Pat couldn't persuade me to wait. I put my clothes on and grabbed some
papers from the desk which might have been important.

"Don't bother calling, I'm going to see a doctor. . . I'll just wait in his
office." I lied.

"Please stay, just for a few minutes while I get my dad on the phone.
Please, Brane."

"No."

"Then I am leaving because there is nothing to do around here except
take care of you and I am not even permitted to do that!" she yelled, ran out.
A few seconds later, the office door slammed.

CHAPTER XIII

As soon as she left, I began to feel slightly better. I was on my feet and feeling somewhat clear, but I hurt all over. There was a momentary remission. After stuffing all those miscellaneous documents into an old leather briefcase, I turned out the lights in the office and struggled to the elevator. As I was walking through the lobby between countless comers and goers, I heard: "Brane, oh Mr. Brane. How are you?"

I turned and saw it was Mrs. Singer, an older woman who worked for an eighty-five-year-old real estate tycoon on the floor below me. Once I had handled a case for her; she had been hit by a full mail sack and I sued the Post Office. She was hellbent on saying hello to me from whatever distance. Sometimes she'd scream at me from the other side of Fifth Avenue during rush hour or I would hear her crackling, high-frequency voice from the corner of a packed elevator car.

I replied, "I'm fine, Mrs. Singer," and tried to get away from her, jerking myself toward the avenue. She pushed through the crowd, sticking her face in mine.

"Where have you been? I haven't seen you in such a long time!"

"Oh, I have been on a vacation . . ."

"Where did you go?" she asked.

"I went out of my fucking mind." Although I tried to retract it, she quickly answered.

"How was it out there, was it lovely?" Her voice went into a singsong tone, trailed off and she left.

A loud bus went by; my head was tied onto its side with a hangman's rope, dangling between two advertisements for vodka. Both of my hands instantly reached for the area on top of the shoulders, meeting one another like they were shaking hands. My God, it was true. I was headless. I tried to feel my chest and legs . . . no sensation, but they were clearly somewhere.

"Go for a walk," I ordered myself. "Walk up Fifth, you'll begin to feel better." At the corner, I was back to normal except there was my head covered with a skintight black hood. It skated right through a red light, made the corner downtown and sped away.

Then it started to rain. Shit, I was afraid I'd be standing in the rain for the rest of the day. For ten minutes I stood on the corner contemplating my destiny, soaking wet. There wasn't a cab in sight—typical city when it rains and no Ubers. You can forget getting a lift. One step at a time, I trudged toward Madison, to a bus stop.

About thirty passengers were waiting. The bus arrived. It was crowded; I had to stand alongside the driver. The sweaty, thick air was suffocating, as if I needed another peril. The last time I rode a bus was years ago. I'd forgotten you need the exact change, not a penny less. All I had was a ten. I tapped the woman sitting in front of me.

"Lady, do you have change for ten dollars?" She looked at me silently. I asked the person next to her and she turned away, thinking I was trying to hit on her. I knew the driver was getting pissed. I yelled out, "Does anyone on this bus have change for ten dollars?"

No answer, that's fucking New York City at its best.

The driver twisted around while we were stopped and warned me, "You'd better get off at the next stop."

Just then, a hand squeezed between passengers extending a five, four ones and four quarters. I exchanged the ten to mystery man and dropped two quarters in the dispenser.

After half an hour we were ten blocks from my apartment. The bus cleared, so I sat in a middle seat and rested my briefcase between me and the next guy. Even though I thought I was fucked up, this bus-load was a reality check: two bickering women, a homeless old man, a drunken cleaning woman laughing hysterically at cell phone cartoons and an Irish MTA cop with a sack of whiskey.

I closed my eyes, wishing and hoping I was anywhere else. But that was impossible. The second I tried to block out the surroundings I lapsed back into the whirlwinds of the craziness, back to the scenes in Radiance's flat, back to Otis driving at me, back to the psychotic garden where there were too many hallucinations for me to digest inside this pit of claustrophobia. I had to watch what was regular in this life, the congestion and the coagulation of the pedestrians transporting themselves home.

When the bus stopped, an advertising guy pushed past me. My briefcase was gone. I glanced around; it was between that guy and a passenger.

I raced to the doors just before they closed, grabbed his collar and pulled him toward me.

"Give me my case, you bastard! Where do you think you're going?"

"Get your hands off me," he caught his breath, straightened himself out and tried to move away. I went for the case just as the bus jerked into gear and humped up Madison, the driver seeming to brake every time one of us would gain an advantage. We wrestled over the case like 2 dogs going at a bone. The case broke open and the papers spilled out. The doors opened and at that moment I let him pull the bag from me when he least expected it. There was nothing behind him except the three steps to the sidewalk. As he tumbled backward, I snagged the case, and watched him roll onto the curb. The doors closed and the bus drove away.

I got down on my hands and knees and picked up all the papers. They were soggy; one of the important contracts had a perfect shoe print on it and the rest were screwed originals. I sat down, started to catch my breath, realized that for those few seconds during the scuffle I wasn't out of my head. I knew everyone was staring at me but I was just fine and got off at the next stop.

The rain didn't affect me, although I was getting very wet, but I was overcome with self-pity. I didn't want to be crazy but I couldn't stop spinning out of control. Who could? Then, I started crying, tears and rain running down my face. I could understand the crying, it was self-pity. Certainly, it couldn't be about Radiance; I was going to see her tonight. That's me the animal spinning around in a never-ending circle, biting my tail, heading toward what was driving me crazy. But I couldn't wait to see her again.

Everything was possible, spreading out, each one a wing, a different thought, aim, ideas ... then it all damn dissipated.

The dry cleaner I used to go to was standing in front of me, closing his shop. I also had a fight with him, years ago, like everyone else over missing buttons or a screwy zipper. Now I had to pick up my favorite necktie I had dry-cleaned. We went inside, he did me a favor, opened the shop and handed me my necktie. He'd shrunk it to the size of chili pepper, then crimped it.

My hand was trembling when I examined it, and I went right to tears.

"That will be $4.50," he demanded. I held the poor little thing in my shaking hand, and whispered,

"You know this was my favorite, cost me fifteen dollars. . . . It was special, I only wore it a few times. It was so beautiful and if you did this to my tie, then you did it to me!" I screamed.

Without any excuse, he barked, "This is the way we received it." The oldest fucking excuse, lie, cop-out in the world.

"You lying prick . . . if there is one thing you did wrong today, it was to get out of your lying bed, come to your lying store . . . you destroyed my helpless tie ... and now you want to get paid for doing it." I grabbed all the laundry bags in front of the counter and threw them onto the sidewalk.

Here I was again in the same place but it wasn't about a necktie.

Well, you can guess what happened—the same thing as Otis and the guy on the bus. The dry cleaner was yet another sentinel telling me I had gone too far. Years later and this fucker was the person in the center of my storm, the closing image of the day. Isn't there a reason for everything, some huge fated master plan, into which I was drawn by the great you-know-who? And if this frump dry cleaner weren't standing in my way, I would have walked calmly home. Anyway, he didn't even know who I was.

When I arrived home, my phone rang. Pat.

"Brane!"

"What is it?"

"Brane, are you feeling all right? I can't see how you're making it."

"Don't worry, my dear. . . . I feel much better." I couldn't feel worse.

"If that's the case then get ready— "

I braced myself, I knew what was coming, another fucking case.

"You know Julian Lopes, he just phoned from the Sixteenth Precinct, busted for armed robbery along with some other guys. A felony."

I was relieved it wasn't a death, pressed my cell to my ear,

"Uh-huh."

"They also got him on a concealed gun. He had a .38, they were robbing a warehouse on Third Avenue and 127th. They'll be arraigned at 100 Centre Street, Part A4. Do you want the phone number of the precinct? 397-6074 . . . if you call, they'll let you talk to him."

"All right."

I called right away.

"Sixteenth Precinct, Sgt. Leslie, can I help you?"

"Yes, Sergeant, this is Mr. Brane, attorney for Julian Lopes"

"Hold it a second, Mac."

For twenty minutes I was on hold. The phone cut out. I tried to call back, but the line was busy. The circumstances didn't give me much choice. Either I could forget it (Lopes had me down as a lawyer since he knew I did criminal defense) or hustle down to the precinct. Don't ask me why I did it; I really didn't like Lopes very much; he was a born criminal and not a nice guy. A few years before, I represented him in a case in Camden, New Jersey, where he went on weekends. He hung out in bars, waiting for someone to take him home.

I shoved the glass door of the station house open. I moved to the intake clerk's counter. The cop behind was busy, grinding his pencil into an open ledger book and I knew from experience not to say a word until he looked up.

"Yes, what is it?"

I handed him my card: "Brane, attorney at law."

"Yes, counselor," he wiped his brow and stuck two fingers into his cheek. "Who's the client?"

"Lopes, Julian . . . booked about two hours ago, robbery. I got to interview him before the arraignment."

"Hold it, I'll check."

About ten minutes later he returned.

"Here's a pass to get back there."

I had to interview Lopes and set the facts.

As I passed each cell, hands, countless hands, reached out to grab on to me: "Hey you, are you my lawyer? Hey brother, gimme a cigarette, come here you white motherfucker."

They didn't tell me which bin Lopes was in, so I had to go down the line.

Once I realized Lopes wasn't there, I quickly returned to the counter.

"Officer, Julian Lopes, do you have him on your roster? He's not there."

"He's not listed; they must have taken him downtown to the courthouse."

"What do you mean?"

His index finger ran along the desk's edge, and he spoke into the papers. "We don't have him, he's at arraignment."

I went to the clerk's office at 100 Centre to get Lopes' papers and to find out exactly what the charges were and when he'd be brought down.

There was a line in the clerk's office; about ten lawyers were in front of me making the same inquiry. Forty-five minutes later, I got to the head of the line. It was the same clerk who had been on night duty since I was a lawyer. No matter what you said to him, it was wrong.

Before I could open my mouth, he yelled at me, "What is it . . . are you a lawyer?"

"Yes, here's my card." Then I remembered I'd forgotten to put on a suit and tie. I was standing there in jeans and a black motorcycle jacket.

"You can't go into court like that, Counselor!" The lines in his brow wrinkled together like a box of worms halfway up his bald head and both of his hands pressed against his temples, like I was hurting his head.

"This case is an emergency. I wasn't in my office when I found out about it and I could not go home to change. I'll explain that to the court. That's not your problem, just go ahead, give me the papers for Julian Lopes. He's been brought in from the Nineteenth. "

"Not my problem, huh!" Saliva flew from both corners of his mouth; luckily, none landed on me. "Not my problem, huh! Not my problem, huh! huh! huh!"

This would go on for minutes, the "huhs" would wind down.

"Stand over there, until I have finished with everyone else . . . then maybe I can find time to look for your client's papers."

"Look," I snapped, "you son of a bitch, you're going to get those papers now! I didn't wait forty-five minutes in line for you to give me a hard time and if you don't . . . "

"Give me the fucking sheet on Julian Lopes!" I yelled.

He looked at me like I was crazy, astonished, and handed me the papers.

As I pushed open the courtroom doors, I began to feel the usual anxiety, not any different from my fear of Radiance. It's all the same. There were about twenty rows of seats. The first and second rows were reserved for lawyers and cops. I moved down the center aisle, staring straight at the bench, careful I wouldn't trip. The judge was berating one of the defendants for not appearing with a lawyer and refusing Legal Aid. I slipped into an empty seat and placed my famous briefcase alongside. I next had to get to the holding cell and interview Lopes. I was attacked by intimidation, butterflies, sent back to the first time I was ever in a courtroom. Whenever I'm in court, I tell myself, "You are a nervous wreck, go ahead and fuck this case up, do it now." It serves to calm me down.

My finger got the bridge man's attention.

"Here are the papers. I am the attorney for Julian Lopes," I whispered to him.

"Are you a lawyer?"

"Yes," I whispered.

"Come with me, around this way." He pointed to the side gate, where the cases are about to be called.

We walked to a door that was to the right of the bench. The judge peered over his glasses, regarding me as if he didn't get where I was going in my outfit.

The fucking jerk didn't realize I was on my way down Violet Avenue. No, I am not dreaming. I am through with the inventory of sadistic melodramas. I am getting out . . . put out like the cat to the yard. There is too much red velvet on Violet Avenue, too much blood, too many times I've rubbed my nose up and then down. I have to maintain this refrain, forget the insulting breakdown, go through the doorway, into the open air. Do I hear my neighborhood friends asking: "Brane, come out and play . . . Mrs. Brane, why can't Brane come out and play? . . . Is something wrong with him? Is he sick or something?" Is the door open wide enough for me to emerge without these fat problems? And just what will I do when I get there? Go to the park.

All of it makes my head roll. I can't leave; I'll solve all of it from here, dying with an empty glass in my hand, writing a memoir. The so-familiar pain in my arms and back now will merge, clash with the effort it took to remember these facts. Yes, of course, that night in the courthouse. It was a joke, well, a joke on me because, in the American way, I didn't get paid. If I leave here, I'll have to get another job and get compensated. This is simple, stay right here and examine each minute event of that life I once lived out of an easy chair. That's correct. I am getting acclimatized, liking it in the hotel. Just because I haven't been put away doesn't mean I am not confined. I'm going, rather, I am staying here, and I'll learn to cook and play the piano. When I am through, I will play great sonatas and eat myself to death. One fantastic disadvantage is that there is nothing to drink, not one thing to coat my mind with while all of this solipsism grows into my last breath before they present Mr. Brane to the embalmer.

Violet Avenue. The only one-way street of the infinite where the straightaway is a trick turn toward myself. The quintessential inquiry, the query which is the parent of the question is: How far can I penetrate the self, the conceited membrane me, the giver and the taker? Does anyone care to take their eyes from what's around them to stare at themselves? No, that would be an admission they no longer were concerned or cared about others. Take my word for it, there are no others. It just looks that way.

How many times have I told myself not to fall for those damn tricks, yes, the ones that got me here like Radiance and the night in the courtroom. All of it, a stupid ruse, agitating on all sides, like competing pieces of sandpaper, one wanting to rub me out faster than the other. But I am more fortunate than most, I was here all the time, no one could reach me any more than the times I'd already been contacted, reached. Now I harbor myself, I don't express the ectoplasmic, the outside actor, to anyone. I dwell in my own interior abode, reek of sweat which I provoke, smell the stench which I manufacture and the absolution of self.

Times are so bad I can't even wash up. For days I've been in these clothes, persuaded that any moment I will rise and change into something clean after a long shower. I have to surmount the fear of leaving, abandoning my bohemian post, the great meditator who brings the outside world into his inner thoughts.

I don't want to venture out, anyway. For what? To find out about those who strive for mediocrity, achieve apotheosis through newspapers, magazines, waves carrying sounds and pictures. Worldliness is for those of the world; I am of this room.

CHAPTER XIV

"The magic number is one," the guard said to me as if I'd known him for years. His belly swung toward the cells, the keys in his pudgy hands clinked; his puffy face lit up like Mercurochrome as he talked about baseball. I kept trying to think of the month; somehow, I thought it was spring.

"Baltimore and Boston are playing tonight. In Boston, they're a tough ballclub," he boasted like a sports announcer, as we passed the first cell.

Baseball, screw that! I hadn't followed any sport since I was fifteen and got interested in girls, although I would collect cards back in the old days. The cop was rubbing his stomach. Supper hour was imminent, ten minutes. His feet were big and flat; his steps sounded like pancakes hitting a frying pan.

"Yankees are losing, 4 to 2, it's the top of the eighth."

I turned from side to side looking for Lopes; there were ten cells to check. While the cop and I were walking, I was again harangued by prisoners hollering to take messages to their old lady, get them a lawyer, warm clothes, bail money, cigarettes, food, dope. I listened because I didn't want them to throw any personal shit my way.

"Baltimore has four games left, so does Boston," he said, wiping his nose with the knuckle of his middle finger.

"If Baltimore wins tonight and tomorrow . . . they could take it 'cause they're in first by a game."

We walked slowly. He wanted to lengthen the analysis all the way to Lopes.

"If Boston," his coaching hand was on my shoulder, "wins and the Yankees lose, then they could win . . . that is, if the Yankees lose the rest of their games. But if the Yankees win, and Baltimore wins tonight, then there could be a three-way tie. No, that's not right . . . there could be a two-way tie. Let's look at it this way: Boston wins tonight and then splits the next two against Baltimore, and the Yankees lose the next three, then Boston and Baltimore could tie, and the Yanks would be out. No, that's wrong, Boston would win by a half a game if Boston wins their last game and Baltimore loses. Baltimore and the Yankees would be tied for second."

With his puppy face he gazed into my eyes and shook his head and conceded,

"Counselor, the Yankees are not going to win!"

"Why?" slipped out.

"Baltimore looks good. Boston has better pitching though. I don't trust that goddarn Boston, but I really think the Yankees can take it." He became hopeful.

I left him standing there, counting on the fingers of his left hand the possibilities of how the teams could finish in the standings, finding Lopes in the next-to-last cell. He spotted me, squirmed through two cons, a brother and the other Hispanic under a Mets cap.

"Brother, I didn't think you'd ever get here!" Two gold-capped front teeth proceeded his words of wisdom.

"Well, I'm here, better get me the facts quick! They're going to call this case any minute!"

"Man, I can't do that . . . it's involved, there are eleven of us. Three guys in the truck, three guys watching for cops and four of us plus me who went inside the joint."

Lopes' nose was running, he wiped it with his wrist and looked around at the other prisoners. He was a good five inches taller than me, had a wide mustache and gold earrings. There was a softness about him, like a muddy trench of disbelief. Every part of his head had been gouged, punched, knifed, pistol-whipped. He never came to my office without a white babe who hung on his arm like he was the black messiah.

Before I answered, I felt sick again. The jail cells fanned by like two high-speed trains passing. Fractions of Lopes' face were talking, each saying different things. At the same time, I sensed I could get Lopes off when we got into the courtroom. About Radiance; she was home congratulating Otis—how he had toyed with me and tried to run me down. I drew a deep breath of anxiety and let it out slowly, carefully.

This wasn't the time to let things run away from the small hold I had on reality.

"Four of you, four of you . . . did you say four of you?"

"What's the matter with you? I haven't got much time. Brane, they're going to call the case any minute. . . . You better listen," he warned me with his index finger touching me and his face pressed between the bars.

If there's one thing I hate, that's it. No client ever warns me about anything . . . especially one that doesn't pay.

"Fuck you, get yourself another lawyer, Lopes. Don't tell me I better do anything. Nothing is wrong with me."

I shot the words at him and snapped myself back into a version of reality. The tendency to do things on the hope, not the actuality, of getting paid was one of my worst qualities. I probably had the largest accounts receivable of any attorney in New York state.

Instantly Lopes apologized, calling me "Bro." Of course, I didn't leave, I'm too soft—never getting mad enough for my own good.

He went on to tell me the story. The four guys outside claimed they were waiting for some friends of theirs. They were going to shoot pool. The four guys in the building had dreamed up a story that they were looking for some Spanish restaurant that was open after hours, and the guys with Lopes each denied they had a gun. The story was bullshit. Lopes and his pals had gone there to rob the place. What the hell were eleven ninjas doing in that building at eleven o'clock at night?

The only thing left was wait, see what happened in the court; maybe the arresting officer wouldn't show, or the complainants wouldn't appear or the district attorney would be incompetent.

"Two games to win, three to tie or two wins and one loss . . . no, that's not right," the guard kept it up.

My eyes looked straight through him as I waited for him to emerge from the sports trance. I stumbled by him and pushed the door open to the courtroom. The place was packed, and I felt like I had walked out on a stage to croon a song in a foreign language I didn't speak in front of a mental hospital. There was about twenty feet between me and the balustrade that separated the seats in the courtroom from the trial well.

The bailiff was next to me. The judge's bench stared at me.

"What are you doing here? You're supposed to be sitting out there, buddy . . . are you a witness?" the bailiff asked.

"No, I'm a lawyer" I didn't say I had a case to present to this court.

"Let me see your card, I've never seen this kind of shit."

"Sorry, I don't carry business cards. You'll just have to take my word for it. I'm an attorney."

"What's your name?"

"Come on, Officer, is this third grade?"

"I don't give a sweet shit who you are, if you don't want to give me an answer ..."

"Julian Lopes, are you represented by counsel in the matter of The State of New York against Julian Lopes?" The clerk read the names of other defendants.

"Brane, glad to see you, we've been standing here for ten minutes," Lopes acknowledged me.

The judge interrupted, "You, in the black leather jacket, are you one of the defendants . . . what's your name? . . . Have you been charged?"

"No, Your Honor, I'm a lawyer, appearing as counsel to defendant Julian Lopes, here on my left."

"Counsel, approach the bench."

"Brane, how are you?" A voice in the back cried out as I headed toward the judge.

Turning, I saw Tom Harris standing there, an ADA from when I was admitted to practice in New York. We passed the bar at the same time.

"Tom, what are you doing here? Don't tell me you're the assistant DA on this case?"

"I am. At first, I didn't believe it was you sitting out there. It's been years since I saw you. Let's get to Levy right away, otherwise he'll throw a shit fit."

"What is the assistant district attorney and Counsel discussing?" Levy barked, as Tom and I walked to the bench.

"Gentlemen, what's this case about? And Counselor, are you dressed for Halloween? Don't you know better? What's your name? Are you, are you in practice for yourself?"

Tom answered, "Judge, he and I know each other for years . . . very honorable counsel, in or out of his motorcycle jacket; matter of fact we went to law school together."

That was a lie, but Tom was going to get me a deal. He worked this courtroom, had been around this judge almost every day for months, whatever he wanted as assistant district attorney would be done. The judge shifted his attention back to me; I could feel Lopes fidgeting his way through the system, uncertain that he'd spend years at Rikers.

"Counselor, I can't understand why you dress like that in court, but that's being overlooked since you're apparently providing a service." Levy's soft bald head hosted a smattering of tiny platinum shrubs that dipped downward where he pretended to read the criminal complaint. His index finger touched his temple, a judicial sign of feigned concentration. I didn't respond, waiting for Tom to take it away.

"Judge, I have reviewed the background of the defendant, Lopes. Although he has a previous record, Class C, there's no evidence that he was in the room when the robbery occurred, he was arrested on the premises but not in the building. The complainant cannot identify him, three men who held them up, they have been identified. They're represented by Legal Aid. Respectfully, I urge the court to reduce the charge to a D misdemeanor, adjourn the case in contemplation of dismissal."

"You think so, Tom?"

"Yes, Your Honor."

"And Counselor, what do you think, will your client plead to a misdemeanor, so we can get rid of this case?"

"I will ask, Your Honor."

I stepped back toward Lopes, the luckiest fucker in NYC, without taking my eyes off Judge Levy. Lopes agreed. The deed was sealed.

CHAPTER XV

It was after midnight when I left the courthouse. Night court was raging. Crime never sleeps in New York. Downtown at that time is as empty as Omaha and not a ride was to be had. From the steps I could see blinking traffic lights and a few cars crawling down Broadway. A crescent moon hung over the West Side's shredded clouds. The pavement rolled toward me and then into the urban folds, and the East River chill reminded me of Radiance. It worried me—had she gone out or was she angry at me for not calling? I wanted her curiosity to work for me, work the impossible, make her come to me.

First order of business, I had to transport myself uptown. I walked down to the piss-laced subway entrance. The rusty metal gates were shut; I'd forgotten that this station closed at 10 p.m. I ran up the steps, overcome with paranoia that I was going to be mugged right against the iron fence down in this hole. Nearly one o'clock in the morning in Manhattan and this was not the place to be. I tried to re-create the fantastic awe I had for the city when I was young. Riding over the George Washington or the Queensboro Bridge, gazing at the city's skyline, thinking someday, yes, I'll actually live here and get to the top. Well, I made it to the bottom. That day was here, and this was me to face and appreciate it.

The city winds howled through me. I stood on the plaza between the federal and state institutions centered in Foley Square. Here was a man on the precipice of yet another breakdown, a term never used by my contemporaries. We freaked and our fathers nervously broke down.

Just perambulate, I told myself, and be rescued by sheer chance. Out of one of those darkened streets a vehicle would appear with a white roof light glowing "Taxi." No, never happened. I was alone and going in goddamn circles. Just then a black car stopped at the corner of Worth and Centre Streets. Two men in the front seat watched me, drove to the curb and parked a few feet away.

The car lurched forward, the dumb ass driver's foot slipped off the clutch. Then the car made four leapfrogs. The motor stalled, the car restarted, shifted into reverse and drove at me. It was Otis and one more creep. I ran across the street, ducked behind the state courthouse to a narrow passageway. They followed me but were unable to drive any farther. I came out the other side to the sound of their disappointed groans.

After a sharp turn, the car drove on the sidewalk and knocked over a trash can. I dashed up Worth, east toward Chinatown. Fortunately, it wasn't far. I darted through the playground and took another right. Shit! A dead end between two buildings. Sweat poured down my back and arms. I stood about a foot from a dead-end alley wall. Waiting. The engine slowed, idling, like a creature stopping to calculate the location of its prey. I tried not to breathe. My heart was racing. I couldn't stop thinking about my legal work, housekeeping and the unpaid bills. Suddenly I was conscientious. I wouldn't finish things, the old items in my desk drawers, and my laundry would never be picked up. Fuck it.

I walked out to the street. The sound of the car echoing in my ears. There it was, not moving, its exhaust seeping into the stoical night. For Christ's sake, why didn't a car drive by or why wasn't there someone in the street?

Some kids were yelling "Good night, see you tomorrow," from Chinatown. Nothing else happened.

The car moved away, picking up speed. Suddenly it raced to the front of the courthouse, roared up Centre Street, lost to the night. I didn't feel any real relief. I counted the butts in the gutter, pulling my arms back and forth, breathing in and out, waiting for the deep fright to dissipate.

I zipped my coat, turned the collar up, knowing the walk ahead was going to be long. Should I phone, tell her I'm on the way? No, the longer she waited the more eager she'll be. She might be angry because I was seriously late for tea.

What about Otis, wouldn't he be there? It didn't matter, seeing her was more important. Do I get one without the other or is it always a package deal? Did she need more intrigue in her life? I concluded confidently, "Yes, I'll provide it" and crossed Canal Street. A cab was pulling away from a neon-trimmed 24-hour diner. I hailed it, and twenty minutes later I was at her doorstep. The doorman unhesitatingly opened the cab door for me. It was after 1a.m.

"Ms. Tempest is waiting, Sir."

I recognized him from the first night. The elevator took me to her floor and I pressed that bell. A maid answered, wearing a starched black-and-gray uniform. Her wrinkled earth-tone skin, sunken cheeks and grooved forehead were intimidating, not inviting.

"Please, sir, Ms. Tempest is expecting you in the drawing room."

After this new maid character brought me into the sitting room, she backed up several old school steps and faded away. The curtains were open, and it all looked the same, the floor-to-ceiling, slanted windows overlooking the reservoir were a set piece—a view setting free the prolepsis of the depth to which I was scheduled to fall this night. I went radio silent. My dry mouth, my chapped lips; how the f could I talk?

Barefoot, Radiance was wearing a long black dress with a mink collar and an onyx necklace. She was so beautiful, so hideously homely—the enemy in the contested territory.

"So lovely to see you, Brane. Would you like to sit down?"

"Yes," I replied but I made no move to do anything. I knew we were not alone, I could feel Otis close by. His presence stirred like squalls over my deck. But I was afraid to lose her attention.

"I wanted to see you today, I wanted to . . . so much. When you didn't come this afternoon, I phoned your office and found out you were in court. Did you win?"

"Yes, if you want to call it that."

I was thinking about Otis and angered that she was pursuing this shallow conversation about court. I wanted to get straight to us, right to why Otis was trying to kill me.

"What about Otis, what he did tonight, running me down and chasing me at the courthouse tonight." I demanded to know what was going on.

"Otis is my friend, much more than that and very possessive. Our lives are centered around one another but I found myself falling in love with you. He is very jealous, he wanted you out of the way. This is an impossible predicament."

She stopped to assess whether I was following her conversation.

"I shouldn't be so vague," she added sweetly, then laughed perniciously.

"I don't understand, Otis is your lover?" Damnit, I hated sounding naive. It made sense that he wasn't a houseboy. Why didn't I figure that out during this blackened week? I turned to Otis, who was laughing, wearing a white suit, just like the one I wore to tea with Hans. Were they staying at the Hotel Randolphe in the room next-door? I was jolted. There was no difference between them and me. The insanity was everywhere. But being with them together was evil, baleful, beyond any containment.

"Why aren't you trying to kill me now?"

"I don't have to, you're no threat." His voice was calm, smart, confident.

"Sir," he uttered in that coffee tone from days ago, "I tried to warn you. This morning! Tonight! But you want to come back! Tell him!"

"None of this really matters. Otis and I will be leaving, probably for good."

"Yes, that's correct. She and I will be going very soon. If it weren't for her having met you, her childish attraction, how ridiculous, how foolish, how maddening, we'll be out of sight, out of your mind," he stammered.

I thought he moved forward, showing her how easily he could overpower me, probably kill me in front of her. But I was unable to detect whether she was in control him or it was the other way around.

"What's it going to be, Radiance? Me or him?"

"I already answered that," she reacted sharply.

"She has told you and understands that you only desire her because what happens here is so out of the ordinary. You're a freak."

"Brane, leave. Forget me!" Her voice was determined, assertive, leaving no room for disagreement or negotiation. But did she want me to go for my own good? The night wasn't going to end without everything in the open, no matter what the price.

"No, Radiance, he won't. He's dumb, can't remember the nights he spent here."

"I know what happened."

"I don't think so," she replied. "It wasn't me making love to you."

"What? I suppose it was Muriel!" I nervously laughed.

"No, but that's not a joke," Otis said.

"Well, let's get it over with. Who was it then, Otis?" I was suddenly realizing the truth.

"Yes, he'd never let me sleep with you. He'd do anything to prevent that, even pretend to be me."

"Or pretend to be unconscious and tied-up," Otis interjected.

"This is stupid, Radiance. Do you think I would, for a second, swallow that? I woke next to you every morning this week."

"And at night?" she asked. "You didn't have any idea of what happened."

I suddenly remembered the feeling, gripping the thighs, the furry, heavy thighs of a monster. The stiff hairs, the feet. They were telling me the truth! The bastards had duped me, but where was she all that time? Goddamn, it made me sick thinking I fucked this diseased creature. I began to turn yellow and green inside, everything was a lie.

"Oh, you thought this was a game, this pursuit. To come after me because I was just another attractive woman, that all the rules of love were going to come into play and ultimately, you'd conquer me, add me to your list."

Then her head swung back and forth as if it were hinged while Otis laughed himself into hysteria.

I could hear that damn beeping again, coming from overhead. Thousands of bats were hanging, brown pouches. There was a sickening odor, then the sound of running water.

The bats were flying, swirling, grouping to attack. They were undeniably gruesome. They explained the moths, the bugs in the kitchen; bats eat them. Radiance fed on them.

I was frightened. No time to think of my old-fashioned values. Radiance's head was disordered, a physically handicapped creature in control. I was their subject.

"Radiance, you . . ." I said, "I must know if it was you or it was him!" Otis burst into savage laughter. Bats were swarming, and each one of the little fuckers had her face.

"Didn't you ever think it could've been Muriel in bed with you and that it wasn't me in the room making all those hideous sounds?"

"Of course not. I know it couldn't have been."

Radiance crossed her legs and placed a book underneath her thigh. She pointed downward. "Your poetry, Brane, took it from your closet."

Otis wasn't laughing anymore, he just stared at me. They were playing with every category of human fear one could endure. I laughed in their faces; this wasn't funny. But I was at their disposal, their slave for any macabre purpose. It was too late, I'd been converted, transmogrified, by them.

Terry couldn't understand my poetry but I never took the time to explain it. She would have understood that it was impossible. How much deeper I was in now. Poetry, shit, poetry; what about these fucking bats clinging to the furniture, to the floor, the windowsill, to my forehead.

I tried to look away from her hands. Her palms were dark, wrinkled, dry. I turned away. She wasn't wearing that dress but she wasn't naked. Her skin was shrinking, each arm was creasing. Her waist, legs and feet were folds of dead skin. Tiny hands protruded that had no connection to her. A fibrous mane grew around her neck. Her ears were red protrusions. Hair grew out from her flattened nose. The teeth were fangs. Her head was fully distorted.

Her nose was wet, flattened, and the rest of that face rain gray. I witnessed the incredible metamorphosis. She was a bat.

"Oh, Brane, how I want to make love to you, but Otis won't permit it!" she shrieked.

"I can't."

This was far beyond what I thought my dull life was about. I tried to run. Toward Otis? My fingers turned gray. I fell to the floor dumbfounded, looking up at her.

Muriel was standing over me.

"What the hell are you doing here?" I asked, gathering myself.

"Brane, I've been here since the beginning, since the night you thought you picked me up. Franco and Magritte don't just throw dinner parties without my consent. I run their show and you're the main character. Isn't that right, Magritte?"

From behind the drapes Magritte appeared holding hands with Franco. It was clear they were fucking card-carrying vampires, fangs, capes and the white-and-red eye shadow.

"Welcome to our world, Brane," Magritte said. "There isn't going to be any horseback riding today, you know, weather. Canceled."

Magritte and Franco walked across the room and stood next to Otis. These actors were in it together and I walked right into the thick of my disaster now playing on Broadway.

Muriel swooped for me, strafing, turning her wings, flying away and returning. Those pulsations, beeping louder with each pass. This was my reality. She slashed at me, caught the side of my face, and tore off a wedge of my cheek.

I crawled to the window, bats blanketing me, crapping all over the beautiful view. Radiance clawed at me, then retreated to the wall, allowing Muriel to have at it.

My clothes were blood-soaked; my face unrecognizable. I saw my hideous reflection, it was a beautiful atrocity. Radiance pulled the bats off as if she were trying to save me.

She swiped at the air, then she was chasing me. Suddenly I thought, fuck it, I would give in, that I was going to lie helplessly flat on the floor, beg for mercy. I would be that person who died because he pleaded for his life.

No, it wouldn't work. I realized what occurred in her bedroom. Radiance revealed herself to me, gave herself in plain sight then. This time I'd make love to her. We'd die in each other's arms. Her leathery neck, would be flush with mine. I ran my tongue along her fangs, pressed it to hers, drank her saliva and then turned to Muriel for a threesome.

I had to get moving, tried crawling toward her, but she was at me first. The bats lacerated my face, arms, chest; her wings covered me like I was a carcass. Just then I was inside her or was it Muriel—both of them were above me, in me or who the f knew where? I pulled my elbows in, tightened my waist, raised my hands to Radiance's neck and pushed my lips against hers, pulled her hideous face to mine. Her fangs raked slivers of flesh from my face, she nibbled away like an alley rat on those rubbery snacks, precisely how she dined at Trick's. The table manners, none of it stopped me. I pulled her mouth to mine, wanting in as far in goes, then Muriel was right there—there was no difference between them.

Shockingly, the energy seemed to transfer from Radiance, then Muriel. I moved Radiance flat on the floor. I smoothed her wings, holding them against her arms. Bloody rivulets coursed down my chest onto Radiance's dark, furry surface. With one hand on her shoulder, the other pulling at my belt buckle, I loosened my trousers. Somehow, I was able to take them off without losing her; she lay quietly, save the thickness of her breath, and waited for me to make love to her, only her. The bats receded, flew back.

Then I was naked. She had nothing on. My fingers touched the inside of her thighs, her withered, fragile, branchlike bones. Her legs and wings moved nervously and stopped. I massaged her boney frame as she lay dying in the classic style of a vampire.

I tried to put myself inside whatever was between her legs. Her tiny fingers barely moved. In every horrible way imaginable she screamed, her legs pulling away, her ears pointing, folding around the base of her skull. She was the woman. Not Muriel. The woman who could rescue me, the one woman I could not have. But I was at the beginning of success.

No, now there would be no others, no turning my head in rooms to see who was coming through the door, no looking down the beach at who was in the bikini, no thumbing through magazines, nothing to look at except her.

I awoke in the morning, alone in Room Thirty-one. There was the number right on the door. My three doctors were standing by my bedside with clipboards. The first one looked just like Radiance, the plastic name tag pinned on her white starched lab coat read, Dr. Radiance Tempest, and alongside her were two other physicians, one was Dr. Magritte Bollane and the other's name tag read Dr. Franco Bollane. They looked happily married. No Muriel; where the hell was she? I could swear Blake was standing on the other side of the room with his hand gripping the door knob.

"Brane, I hope you didn't go to the country this weekend. I heard the weather was terrible," Dr. Tempest said.

"Oh no, Doctor, I hate it when it rains, then I just stay in the hotel and watch the chestnut trees sway back and forth. My favorite is looking out my window, it's a beautiful landscape painting out there, as you know, weren't most landscape painters institutionalized?"

"Art is not something I have time to appreciate, but you often tell me about sculpture and paintings you like, that's impressive, I do like old masters," Dr. Tempest replied and when she replied her old her face rapidly aged and morphed into an ashen tone.

The old woman and Otis were gone, and the other cast of characters gave me something to think about. Weren't they coming back?

Besides I had just walked over from Violet Avenue; I went to the drugstore to get toothpaste and light bulbs and I didn't feel like going anyplace else. But I also went to the office and called Radiance. A man answered and insulted me. We argued, then he told me to call back when she returns. How will I know when? Every time I call Radiance, that man answers the phone. Radiance is always out. What can I do? I'll go down Violet Avenue, I can reach her there.

THE END